BEYOND THE MOUNTAIN

Mark Higgins

Fisher King Publishing

Beyond The Mountain

Copyright © Mark Higgins 2023

Paperback ISBN 978-1-914560-71-2
Ebook ISBN 978-1-914560-72-9

All rights reserved.

Published by Fisher King Publishing

www.fisherkingpublishing.co.uk

To my wife Morag for her constant
support and guidance, without which
this book would just have been an idea.

Chapter One

Sounds of the city coming to life filter through the open window. On a side table, a sunlight alarm clock blinks on and intensifies with every passing minute. A woman's hand jolts from under the covers and fumbles for the off switch. Rising, Professor Alex McDonald sits on the edge of the bed, she switches her mobile on, checks her messages, then walks towards the bathroom door. The small room is clouded with steam. Alex wipes the mirror, her finger traces a crescent shaped scar above her left eye, she thinks back to the accident that caused it.

The massive white cornice of ice cascades down a vertical slab of rock; its surface glimmers with an iridescently blue in the cold winter sun. Two small brightly coloured dots move cautiously up the treacherous icy curtain nearing the summit. Alex removes her gloves, tucks them inside her bright blue padded jacket. She retrieves a small energy bar from a pocket and opens it. High above her, Gordon Smith looks down at Alex and laughs to himself. "Hey McDonald, you stuffin your face, again?" Alex smiles.

"I missed breakfast." She shrugs her shoulders.

"First rule of climbing Alex, eat your fucking porridge." They laugh.

Gordon kicked hard at the ice with his crampons, there's a deafening noise above them, like a clap of thunder. He instinctively looks up and calls out in fear. "Avalanche!"

Alex grabs the handles of her axes and swings them hard, burying each jagged head deep into the ice wall above. She watches on in horror as Gordon is torn from the ice. His body disappears inside the boiling torrent of snow that continues its relentless descent towards her position. The massive impact rips Alex from the mountainside; her body falls a hundred feet before smashing into the unforgiving rock face. The huge impact leaves a large, incised wound above Alex's left eye. She hangs motionless beneath an overhang, blood pouring freely from the nasty gash and drips into the void below. Gordon's broken body lies lifeless, partially buried in avalanche debris on the glen's floor.

Chapter Two

Alex unconsciously rubs the scar above her eye before switching the shower off. She returns to the bedroom in a bathrobe sitting and drying her hair with a towel. Her phone rings, she picked it up, puts it on speaker. "George what can I do for you?" Alex continues to dry her hair.

"Hi Alex, sorry to bug you at the weekend. I know you're going to the cottage today and wondered if you could do me a wee favour?" Alex rolled her eyes.

"Sure, what is it?" She put the towel on the end of the bed, brushing her hair back with her hands. "You still there George?"

"Yes, it's a bad line I think. Anyway, there's been some unusual seismic activity in the glen overnight and I wondered if you could have a quick look, see?" Alex picked up the phone, walks to the kitchen, switches the kettle on.

"That fine, I'm going up there anyway but don't hold your breath for anything special that volcano's been dead for years." She laughed to herself.

"Great, thanks Alex much appreciated, see you soon bye." The line goes dead before she can reply. Alex shakes her head and sits the phone down. She makes herself a coffee, walking to the window and looking at the dark waters of the Clyde. They always seemed to remind her of Willy Wonka's chocolate river. Finishing her coffee, Alex dressed quickly, lifting the pre-packed bergen sitting by the door. She has one last look around the apartment then leaves.

Chapter Three

Alex looked up at the imposing figure of Buachaille Etive Mor (The Shepherd of Etive Moor), a mountain guarding the entrance to Glencoe and the valley beyond. Sunlight bathes its easternmost flank in soft yellow light, illuminating the greens, browns and grey-purple hues where vegetation and the near-vertical rock face collided. Continuing her journey along the valley floor, she looked up at the peaks that dominated the surrounding area. She could see how much time and the elements had battled to erode the magnificent landscape.

Alex still held the title to her grandparents' property outside Glencoe village where she had grown up following the untimely death of her parents in a tragic accident. For part of the year the cottage was a holiday let, affording her a substantial extra income that helped to pay for its maintenance. She did, however, always manage to find time each year to take a break from the hustle of city life to visit and keep the edge on her mountaineering skills, which in her line of work were a necessity. Her thoughts were brought back to the task at hand when she noticed quite a sizeable rockslide at the base of the northside of the mountain. 'Not a waste of time after all.' She thought. Hurrying towards the debris field. Glencoe had been the site of a super volcano and the valley beyond its caldera, (magma chamber), but that had been millennia ago. Only normal seismic activity had been recorded in the area and nothing big enough to cause this amount of movement. Taking out a rather ornate pocket watch, she marveled at the exquisitely carved outer case done in an Art Nouveau style. The watch, along with the cottage and some of her guardian's paperwork, were all that was left of her clan's history which, like the watch case itself, were etched in time. Most Scots were aware of the story of the Massacre of Glencoe, but her grandfather had told her there was more to the tale than met the eye. Pressing the catch on the side of the watch, the lid flipped open to reveal an equally exquisite interior, carved in runic symbols. The watch face looked as new as the day her grandfather had made it, the hands telling her it was eleven fifteen. She cast a final admiring eye over the precious heirloom then slipped it back inside the inner pocket of her jacket.

Alex re-set her backpack and walked on. It didn't take her long to reach the debris field, which was even more impressive up close. Some of the rocks must have weighed five to ten tons. Again, she was bathed in sunshine. Just at that moment, something caught her eye further up the debris field; it was shining. 'It can't be…' Alex thought, picking up the rock. Sure enough, it was a piece of gold. The nugget was about the size of the end of her thumb and smooth, unlike other gold nuggets she'd seen, which tended to be quite rough. There was a goldmine just outside the village of Tyndrum about thirty miles further south that had just recently re-opened, but nothing had been found this far north. Given the look of it, Alex thought it must be man-made. She popped the nugget into a small container resembling the kind you used to get when you bought a reel of film for a camera, in the good old days before everything went digital. With that done, she walked back to the cottage. Later that day she made her way back to the busy lights of Glasgow and her appointment with a fine single malt.

Chapter Four

Like Alex's grandfather, Jim McLaughlin was a craftsman. As an artisan jeweler of some note for high-end clients worldwide. Jim had on occasion made a few pieces for childhood friends and close family. Looking at the nugget, he had agreed with Alex that the gold had been worked before. "Where d'you get this again?"

"My boss sent me to Glencoe as apparently there had been some unusual seismic readings. Turns out the old sod was right. Anyway, I'm in the middle of this huge debris field when the light catches *that*." Jim frowned, turning the nugget over in his hands. "I still don't know how it ended up out there."

Full of excitement, Alex continued, "Anyway, I've always fancied a fob for my grandfather's watch, wondered if you would mind making it for me, please?" Jim looked at Alex for a second.

"Since it's you, fine, but it'll cost you for the chain, mates rates and that." The two friends shook on the deal.

With a perplexed "damn", the jeweler scratched his head. "You're going to burn, my friend!" Jim speaks to the nugget in a one-sided conversation. He reached for the control knob on his mini smelter and turned it to maximum.

The melting process took three times as long with twice the heat but he finally got the job done. He had been surprised, not only by the purity of the gold but also that there was no waste material when he smelted it. Alex had left her watch as Jim wanted to copy some aspects of the design to his piece. He'd always marveled at the craftsmanship and was in awe at the patience, skill, and time it must have taken to produce a watch of such rare quality.

When it came to the etching of his piece, though, it was a whole different ball game. Jim managed to get it to the correct size but he'd broken countless tools trying to work it, eventually deciding that Alex would have to have just a plain old-fashioned one. If she wasn't happy, she could go to hell. Jim caught his last thought. He'd noticed that over the last few weeks since he had started work on Alex's piece, his usual easy-going manner and go-with-the-flow persona were in short supply. Clients, suppliers, and friends alike had felt the wrath of his unusually short temper. "This bloody thing is cursed, no wonder they burned it and left it in the middle of nowhere!"

Surprised by the venom in his words, he picked up his mobile phone and scrolled down till he found Alex's number.

Alex stood in Jim's workshop wondering what had happened to her friend. "Buddy, you need to calm down. If I knew it was going to cause this much trouble, I wouldn't have brought it to you!" Alex was surprised by how upset her friend was. Having known Jim all her thirty years, she had only seen her friend this angry on two previous occasions and on both Jim had been drunk.

After about five minutes, the two friends had calmed down and were enjoying a strong cup of tea. Jim was telling Alex about some of the antique pieces he'd worked on in the past that he was sure had negative feelings attached to them. Having heard these stories before, Alex sat quietly and let her friend retell them, which seemed to have a calming effect on Jim.

Getting back to the piece Alex had commissioned, Jim went to his safe and removed a small red velvet bag. Alex was excited and could not wait to see what was inside. Jim opened the bag and let its contents slip onto the counter. "I know that this is not what you asked for, but it felt right for the piece!"

Alex looked at her friend's eyes; he seemed to be somewhere else. Glancing down, she picked up the rectangular amulet, etched in old runic symbols similar to her grandfather's watch.

"Jim, it's beautiful and the chain's perfect." She places the piece back in the pouch and put it in her pocket. Jim handed back Alex's watch.

"You look after yourself. Be careful with that fuckin' thing, I'm tellin' you, it's cursed!" Alex looked at her friend's face and found no humour.

"Thanks, buddy, I'll transfer the money I owe you later."

"Yer money's no good here. You can name a fossil after me if you want." Alex smiles.

"You're not that old are you." They laugh. The friends shook hands one final time. Jim stood in the doorway and watched Alex's figure till she disappeared out of sight.

Back at her flat, Alex looked down at the pendant. She had never really been a fan of jewelry and in her line of work it was probably more of a hindrance than a help. She made a mental note to remove it before climbing.

Chapter Five

It was coming up to the time for Alex's annual leave. She had already decided to go back to the cottage and sort through some of the paperwork that had been left by her grandparents. She found it hard to believe that it had already been ten years since she lost her grandfather and she still felt it had almost certainly been related to the passing of her grandmother the year before. She had avoided doing anything with her grandparents' documents, simply securing them away in a part of the cottage, the attic, which no one had access to but her. It was on his previous trip north that she thought it was time to move forward, to put things in their rightful place. With a final look back into the flat, she set the alarm and secured the door.

After climbing into her Toyota four-wheel drive, or as she lovingly called it, 'The Go Anywhere Mobile', Alex glanced down at the amulet hanging round her neck. The sight of it unconsciously drew her thoughts back to the dreams she'd been having over the last few weeks. She would not call them nightmares, but they'd still been vivid enough to unnerve her and over time they had become more detailed in intensity. The strange thing was that the dreams all had a common theme, a dark shadowy figure, and a featureless void of black menace.

Alex left Glasgow heading north. Not long into the journey, she started to think about her grandfather. What had the old man meant when he told him there was more to the story of the Massacre of Glencoe? Maybe the answer was locked in the attic in the cottage.

She stopped as always at the cafe just outside the village of Callander. There she sat watching the hustle and bustle in the popular tourist spot, occasionally quietly laughing at the canteen staff's attempts to communicate in four different languages at equally loud volume. 'Well, if they don't understand you, they sure as hell won't miss you,' she thought to herself, a broad smile on her face.

As she made her way back to the pick-up, Alex stopped to talk to Angus the resident Highland bull, whose face could be found on various keepsakes in the gift shop attached to the cafe. After saying her goodbyes to Angus, she drove on.

It took her another two and half hours with one more stop to purge her body of the morning's fluid intake before she turned onto the single-track road that led up to the cottage. After fishing the door key out of her pocket, Alex pushed it home as she'd done so many times over the years. Always travelling light, she'd managed to pack all her belongings for the next two weeks into one hold-all. Decanting her clothes into the small antique chest of drawers and wardrobe set into the wall, she could still feel the presence of her grandparents as if they were going to walk through the door at any moment.

There was no point in starting anything this late, so she reached into her hold-all and pulled out a bottle of Jurra single malt, named after a small island off the west coast of Scotland. Unlike a lot of her kinsmen, Alex savoured her malt rather than using its anesthetic properties to obliterate the day's woes. "THEY BELONG TO ME!"

Alex sat bolt upright. It took her a few seconds to get her bearings. The only light source in the room was coming from the dying embers that were left of the fire she'd lit earlier. She found the main light and flipped the switch. 'Ok, calm down, think logically,' she told herself, 'It was just a dream, wasn't it?'

The following day, Alex sat at the kitchen table eating her breakfast, trying to work out the previous night's events. Must have been the malt, she guessed, but she had drunk no more than her limit of two glasses, so what had caused that voice? Eventually putting it down to tiredness from the journey north, she ascended the straight stairs to the attic.

In a cottage this size, the attic was small and as she stepped through the hatch she barely had enough room to stand up, choosing eventually to stay bent over at the waist. She quickly found what she'd been looking for; her grandfather's oak chest. She sat the great box in the middle of the living room floor, fumbling through the set of master keys that she had brought with her till she found the one that was needed. With an audible clunk, she finished turning the key. Putting a hand either side of the lid, she lifted it to reveal the treasure within; a few family heirlooms and the documents she'd come to look through.

Alex found the master copy of the deeds to the cottage and the modest piece of land it sat on. There were countless ordinance survey maps showing most of Scotland's highest peaks. Her grandfather had taught her all she needed to know to survive in the harshest conditions the seasonal weather could muster. There was also her family tree, marriage certificates for both her grandparents and, of course, for her mother and father. This task was becoming more difficult than she'd thought it would be. Being just an infant when she lost her parents, Alex only had faded memories of their time together. With tears rolling down her face, she was angry about losing her composure. "Get your shit together!" She shouted at the room, but there was no comfort echoed back to her. Wanting to shut the lid, Alex continued to do what she'd been secretly dreading for years – confront her past.

Chapter Six

'If they only knew the truth.' Tom Johansen thought, passing through the strict security protocols forced on everyone involved in any type of research at the CERN facilities. Apart from the now world-famous Large Hadron Collider, which was vast, the complex was comprised of countless labs, lecture rooms and a small but highly skilled security garrison, not counting the sleeping quarters, administration and recreational buildings and restaurants. It was towards this building that Tom was heading.

American by birth but of Nordic decent, the scientist made a striking figure; six foot six with blonde hair and piercing blue eyes on top of a well-built frame, attributes passed down from his Norse ancestors. He strode with the confidence of a man with a purpose. He had passed out of Cal Tech Summa Cum Laude with a doctorate in particle physics before studying under the renowned British physicist Professor Brian Fox for a further three years until he was accepted for a teaching position with CERN. His field of study was dark matter, a relatively new area of research in which he was only one of a handful of pioneers studying the effects on the cosmos of this mysterious entity.

Tom passed quickly through the restaurant only talking when having to exchange pleasantries with the girl at the check-out. On entering his office, he placed the bottle of water and the salad he'd bought on the table, leaving them for a moment to boot up his computer to check yesterday's results, which were disappointing. They showed the same outcome as all the other fifteen days he'd been running this simulation. "Jesus Christ!" he spat the words through his teeth.

He hit 'Retry' on the computer screen, which buzzed into

life like a swarm of angry mosquitoes. 'One more week,' he thought. "I'll give it one more week." Tom was surprised that he had spoken out loud.

After lunch, he did his usual rounds, both in person and electronically. After the discovery of the Higgs boson or God particle, there had been a real jump in the amount of funding being released for research. There were also more eager young scientists wanting to not only study in this field but also to use the facilities and run their theories, which had thrown a metaphorical spanner in the works.

By nature, Tom wasn't the most social individual on the planet, feeling quite at home in his own company and only interacting with colleagues and students when he deemed it necessary. Today was one of those unfortunate times. Putting on a brave face, he shifted into his other persona with chameleon-like grace. Opening the door, he entered the lab with a hearty, "Good morning.", which sounded believable even to him. After the formal introductions were over, Dr Johansen got down to business.

When he'd finished with the students, he then went to check the rota for use of the collider, having booked some time in advance over six months ago. When he looked, there were only two weeks left till the next series of his experiments, but that all depended on the results of the simulation running on his computer at that very moment. *He* depended on it; Tom wasn't talking about himself.

Chapter Seven

There it was, scattered over the living room floor – her past. Alex looked through some old family photos from her childhood. She could vaguely remember some of it but a lot had been blotted out by the passing of time. The brain has a good self-defense system and, being only a child back then, Alex thought that it must have buried those memories deep. She had decided to give some of the heirlooms to the family she had left, feeling like it was the right thing to do; she always went with her intuition. Her family tree could be framed to hang on the wall in the flat. The birth certificates would stay with the box. Any legal stuff, such as the deeds, would also go back to Glasgow with her.

Reaching inside the chest to put the documents back, her thumb brushed a small button set into the lock mechanism. She'd never noticed this before because it looked like a screwhead and having only been in the chest on two previous occasions, she wouldn't have thought to look for it. A small drawer popped out at the bottom right-hand side of the chest. Inside were two yellowed letters, both with her name on them. One she could see was in her grandfather's handwriting. Setting this letter to the side, she picked up the other one and turned it around in her hand, her mind racing at this new development.

Alex was on her knees in the back garden of the cottage, sobbing uncontrollably with the open letter in his hands, it read:

Our dearest Daughter,
On reading this letter, we will be long dead. We want you

to know you are the most precious gift that we were so lucky to have. Also by now you will be of age to know the truth about our history and the reason you are here and why we were murdered.

That last word hit her square in the chest as though she'd been punched by some unseen hand. Struggling to breathe, she continued to read.

For centuries, your kinsmen have been guardians of a great secret and warriors to protect that secret from the hands of those who would use that power to summon the Darkness. We have protected this realm for millennia and in all that time our people have faced famine, persecution, and death, all in the name of freedom, a freedom from a darkness that would consume not only our realm but the others who stand in line against the blackest foe.

The more she read, the more she felt as if her life was spiraling out of control.

We hope that your grandfather has prepared you for that day, the day we hope never comes, when you follow in the path of your bloodline and use your keen mind and warrior spirit to take up arms against the biggest threat to not only our realm but the others you must explore. It was our only wish that you would never have to read this, but if you do, we want you to know that you will always be our only love, our precious daughter. Keep your mind as sharp as your blade and your heart as warm as the sun.

Your ever loving parents xxx

Standing, Alex's jeans were soddened from the morning dew, she wiped the tears from her eyes and tried desperately to refocus her thoughts back to normality. Moving back into the cottage she stood in the kitchen of her childhood home, which at that moment in time felt very alien to her. "Is this happening? Who am I? Is this real? Why were they murdered?" The words bounced off the walls and headed out of the door, leaving her with no answers to her current situation.

Making her way into the small home in a daze she sat in a chair staring at the chest. Her grandfather was a keen practical joker but if this was a joke, it was in bad taste. As she opened the letter from her grandfather, she half expected to see the paper covered with the words 'gotcha', but this of course was just wishful thinking. On unfolding the sheets of paper, Alex looked down at the familiar penwork. The old man had always used a fountain pen in all his correspondence and this note was no different.

My dear lass,

If it were my choice, you would have known what I'm about to tell you a long time ago, but it wasn't. Likewise, if you feel any ill will towards me, that would be completely understandable. It was not my intention to deceive you, quite the contrary. I wanted to prepare you for what you are about to face.

'Was this the same man who raised me?' Alex thought, then continued.

You will hopefully now know why I pushed you so hard to be self-sufficient and able to take care of yourself in the most dire of circumstances. The enemy you face is ancient. It was born in the blackness at the beginning of time and has only one purpose; to obliterate all life. Through the ages, warriors from all the realms have battled to keep it at bay. These warriors include your kinsmen. The McDonalds are not only guardians of this knowledge but are also protectors of this realm and every fifty years, a warrior is chosen to be trained. On the coming of their 30th year, they will be given the knowledge of their ancestors.

It was now becoming clear why Alex had been pushed to excel in martial arts and taken on all those winter climbing expeditions where they had to live off the land and their wits.

Along with this letter, you will find a couple of other documents detailing things you must find and places you must go. There is also a copy of the blueprints to the pocket watch, which I hope is still in your possession. Read them carefully as there is more to that watch than first meets the eye.

She sat for a moment open-mouthed; 'this couldn't be true, it just…' She read on.

Finally, lass…

There were large blotches on the paper where her grandfather's tears had smudged the scroll.

I know that these letters will have changed your whole world but believe me, if there was any other way we could have told you the truth we would have. I have always loved you as if you were my own and I know your dear grandmother felt as I did, that you are kin but so, so, much more to us. We cherished every moment spent with you and our only wish is that we could have spared you from the journey ahead.

Farewell, our precious one. 'Keep the sun at your back and the wind in your face till we meet again in the next life.'

With these final words, her grandfather was gone. "No, no, no…" Years of pent-up grief flooded through Alex's entire being. Never in her life had she felt so alone, so helpless.

After what seemed like an eternity, she managed to get herself focused. Although the letters had affected her very deeply, they had also managed to bring some clarity to different areas of her past life. With that, she picked up the papers that had been left by her grandfather and read on.

Chapter Eight

In his private quarters in CERN, Tom Johansen woke from a nightmare. "IT'S NOT READY!" he shouted to a faceless menace that had pursued him back to this world. Sitting on the edge of the bed, he tried to gather his thoughts. Being a scientist, he didn't believe in an afterlife, let alone the boogeyman. Over the past nine months, however, the boundaries between fact and fiction had, to him, started to merge.

Ever since the triumphant Higgs boson experiments, Tom had been experiencing a change in his beliefs. It was shortly after the amazing discovery of the God particle that he began hearing the voice. He had at first put it down to overworking in the lab but very quickly realized that it was something quite different when 'the voice' began telling him things, details that only he could understand. At that point, Tom had become a disciple of The Darkness, the necromancer.

He paced the length of his open-plan room, which consisted of a kitchen, a bed, a television that he never used and a wet room. The only mod-cons he had were his laptop, a top-of-the-range mobile phone that he only used in emergencies, and, of course, the air conditioning unit that made life there just about bearable. Tom headed for the laptop and touched the keyboard, watching the screen flicker to life. It confirmed his suspicions with the words 'Attempt Failed' across its flat surface. Letting out a long sigh, he changed a few characters and maneuvered the cursor to the icon that said 'Retry', tapping the enter key before he went to prepare for the day ahead.

Chapter Nine

Alex looked up at the grey slab above her then over at the clouds kissing the top of the Three Sisters of Glencoe. She knew from experience that when the mist came down this far, it was time to go. Knowing the next pitch like the back of her hand, she worked out that there was just enough time to finish her assent and abseil down before the elements took hold. Well, that was her plan. In the past if there were any problems in her life, she would head for the mountains, finding that the solitude of climbing had a positive effect on her psyche and that being out in the elements was extremely therapeutic.

She continued climbing, following a natural crack in the rock face, and locking her line into the carabiners as and when needed. Nearing the top, she locked herself off to give her body a rest from the lactic acid levels building in her muscles. Leaning away from the slab, she shook her arms trying to work the tension out.

Anchoring the rope for the decent, Alex noticed a mist rolling downward over the cliff like some ungodly tsunami. She'd been caught out by the weather before, but this was different; there was a feeling of menace that she'd never felt on a climb before. She hurriedly attached herself to the abseiling rig and started down. The only reference point was the small part of the slab she could see. Her rope, all other landmarks and the light had been obliterated by the thickening fog. For the first time in a while, she was scared.

Abandoning her well-drilled technique, she headed down fast, feeling nauseous and cold. It could be trauma from the fall, but her gut was telling her a different story; she felt like she was being hunted. At that moment, Alex crashed into the debris field at the bottom of the slab. The impact knocked the wind out of her, and she struggled to take in air. Getting to her feet, she pulled out her knife and cut herself free from the rope, which fell in tangles at her feet. Now running, she was in complete survival mode and still had the knife firmly in her hand. The cloud broke just in time as she was only meters from a hundred and fifty foot drop to the river below. Standing on the precipice, she got her breath back then looked back up the mountain, now bathed in glorious sunshine. Gathering her thoughts, she continued down the mountainside and onward to the welcoming sight of the cottage.

As a geologist, Alex had been taught to follow evidence. After the previous day's drama, she decided she would look at the documents her grandfather had left her to see if there was any truth in what was written. She read through them, noticing countless dates and events where it was alleged that her kinsmen had held their foe at bay. Of course, the most famous date, 13th of February 1692, was the famed Massacre of Glencoe during which one hundred and twenty men led by Robert Campbell of Glen Lyon killed many members of the McDonald clan whilst staying as guests in their homes. What happened, according to the history books, would go down in infamy.

The soldiers were ordered to slaughter their hosts. Some of them told the McDonald clan what was happening, while others broke their swords rather than break the centuries-old accord of hospitality where, friend or foe, whilst under a host's roof you were his guest and treated as such. The blame for this treachery fell at the feet of Secretary of State John Dalrymple, who alleged that the clan McDonald had refused to swear allegiance to the king. In reality, the order was given by King William of Orange, who had lost one of his generals at the Battle of Prestonpans and wanted revenge on the unruly

Scots. Most of this tale was true, but it was who had influenced Dalrymple where the story got on track. The then Secretary of State had sworn allegiance to the Darkness. As a result, Alex's kin were ordered to scatter to the winds, leaving only a small band to carry on the fight in their homelands. Alex was astounded at how far back this battle had raged. The more she read, the more she began to see the truth that lay in front of her about her clan's history. She turned her attention to her grandfather's watch.

Not being mechanically-minded, Alex did her best to make sense of the drawings now covering most of the kitchen table. She'd thought about asking Jim, but after the incident with the nugget, she'd ruled that idea out. Maybe her old friend Hector could help her. Hector Keegan was, like Alex, a mountaineering geek. As luck would have it, Hector was also a bit of a photography buff and could repair most things to do with his cameras and any other mechanical device that took his fancy. The last Alex had heard, Hector was teaching ice climbing at the indoor mountaineering centre at Kinlochleven, which as luck would have it was only eight miles away in the town of the same name.

"Sorry, Hector hasn't worked here for the last six months. I think the last anyone heard of him, he was working as a guide doing photographic tours of the Pyrenees. Why don't you ask his sister, Jade? She's the one who got his job here."

To be fair, Alex hadn't bumped into Hector for a while, let alone his little sister Jade. The guy pointed Alex to the far side of the building where she could see the back of a girl who was having an animated discussion with an extremely tangled piece of climbing rope. "I'm looking for a climbing lesson," Alex asked.

"Unfortunately, you'll have to come back tomorrow, sorry,"

Jade replied, not looking up from her current predicament.

"That's some attitude you got," Alex said, trying to bait her. It worked. Jade rounded on her.

"Alex McDonald?" She said with a quizzical tone in her voice, then threw her arms around her in a friendly embrace.

"How long has it been, five, maybe six years?"

With a smile breaking across her face Alex returned the hug. "Think it's nearer six! You've grown since the last time I saw you."

"You would have noticed if you had been around." She smiled as she spoke.

"To many memories, that and life, it all catches up with you." They laughed.

"Fancy a coffee and a catch up?" Jade asked.

"Sounds like a plan." Alex smiled at her and they headed for the exit.

The tearoom and gift shop sat between Glencoe and the village of Ballachulish. The main front part was reserved for gifts and clothes for the tourist trade with the cafe at the back. After saying good morning to the girl on the till, it was to the rear of the building that they headed. The cafe was built into an extension with a high vaulted ceiling supported by sturdy beams that came together at a central point, giving the effect of a spider's web. "What's your poison?" Alex asked.

"Cappuccino, please," Jade smiled.

Jade grabbed a table at the far end of the room whilst Alex stood in the queue waiting to be served. She sat watching her goof around, thinking to herself what a beautiful woman she was and that she'd kept herself in shape. Thinking back to when she was younger, she did have a bit of crush on her, but she was Hector's friend, so had kept it to herself. Finally, Alex was served and headed back in her direction. Again, Jade took in Alex's frame, with her dark hair and hazel eyes; she did stand out from the crowd. Placing the tray on the table, Alex took off her jacket, put it on the back of the chair, then sat down. "What's so amusing?" She asked, sorting through the tray's contents.

"You," Jade replied, trying to keep the grin off her face and failing. "You are just the way I remember."

"Well, I hope that's a good thing," Alex said, fishing for another compliment.

Their eyes locked for a moment, then both found solace in their respective beverages. Alex sat sipping her tea and momentarily taking in the various paintings displayed on the walls. There were some of the glen and others of 'The Shepherd' from a different angle, along with pictures of other landscapes that she didn't recognize. She was snapped out of her daydream when Jade asked, "Penny for your thoughts?"

"Sorry," She replied. Jade asked again. Alex apologized once more for getting distracted. "This place hasn't changed, still has a good vibe."

"Yes, it's always the place to come if you're having a bad day. You can just relax here and watch the world go by. What brings you back to this neck of the woods?" Jade quizzed.

Alex told her everything about her job, being sent up here, and all that had gone on previously up to the point of bumping into her again.

"Are you going to let me see these blueprints?" Jade asked.

Alex did a visible doubletake.

"You don't think I'm crazy then?" She said with a puzzled look on her face.

"Yes, I do think you're crazy, but then again you always have been." She laughed.

Jade continued, "I've always had an open mind and if a spaceship landed there in the car park, it wouldn't surprise me, not one bit." At this, they both burst out laughing, relishing each other's company. After lunch, they arranged to meet later when Alex would let her have a look at the blueprints.

Chapter Ten

Tom looked at his laptop screen; it read, 'Simulation Successful'. He fought back tears of joy, falling backwards onto the bed. It was his own private 'eureka' moment but only he and his dark mentor would be privy to the success of the experiment that he was about to initiate. His plan, if executed correctly, was to open a large enough portal to this realm for his lord to be able to push though and exact death and destruction on a global scale. What the good doctor was forgetting was that he was part of this realm and therefore would be held accountable the same as anyone else. But Tom had been blinded by the necromancer's lies, continuing to do his bidding on the promise of power and unlimited wealth. His lord had many names in many tongues; Necro monger, the Darkness, Legion, and in this realm, his common name was Satan.

Tom was growing closer to the culmination of his life's work, or so he thought. For him, the nights were that of a tortured man as his very soul was bartered for by the forces on both sides in this ultimate field of battle. At the start of each day, he lost just a little more control of what he valued the most, his intellect.

"Not long to go now, not long to go now, you'll see, YOU'LL SEE WHO HAS ABSOLUTE POWER!" He did not realize that he was screaming this at the top of his lungs. It was a good job the rooms were soundproofed.

Having run the simulation twice with the same result, he checked the Rota again. It told him there were ten days to go. He smiled then disappeared to his lab.

Chapter Eleven

Alex drove through Glencoe village; she couldn't get her mind off Jade. She arrived at the cottage in five minutes, parked the car and got inside just as the rain started. It had been quite a long time since she'd seen Jade and she had become a very mature and attractive young woman with a great sense of humor. They had agreed to meet for a meal at the local hotel where she would show her the blueprints. Gathering the documents together, she noticed some faint writing on the back of them. Taking a closer look under the light, it looked like a riddle.

To the glen that once was hidden,
I must do a clansman's bidding.
The key is in the clock,
All answers there to mock.
Open the gate to another place,
To protect the land's abundant grace,
Look first to the Gatekeeper.

Alex scratched her head and read the rhyme again. She figured it was to protect her legacy but could only guess a few parts of it. 'Maybe Jade could shed some light on it?' She thought.

Jade's mind was a blur. She still couldn't believe how things had turned out. She felt very at home is Alex's company, as did Alex in hers. It felt easy. The things she had told her, there were many tales of strange goings on in the glen; was this any different to them? Being an architect, she felt that her background would give her some insight into the workings of the watch and there was always Hector; all she would need to do is fax him the drawings and she was sure he could come up with an answer.

During the drive to the hotel, Alex thought in a slightly panic, 'Am I underdressed?' Her idea of dressing up was putting a blouse on with her jeans, which is exactly what she was wearing. 'It's not a date, it's not a date, we're just two friends catching up and having a meal whilst trying to work out what my time-travelling grandfather's magic watch does.' Listening to a favorite track on the radio, she tapped out the beat. Suddenly, the feeling was back, that deep uneasy feeling she had had on the mountain. Gunning the engine till she was just outside the village, she turned left into the petrol station. Alex didn't really need fuel but knew there would be someone on duty at that moment. Once the feeling had passed, she continued her journey towards the hotel.

She'd arranged to pick up Jade at the tearoom on the way to dinner. Turning into the car park, she was immediately relieved to see that Jade had decided to dress casually too in a plain top, jeans with flat shoes. "You scrub up well for a climbing bum," she teased.

Jade smiled, did a quick twirl, then got into the passenger seat. Reaching over, she planted a friendly kiss on her cheek.

"I'll take that as a compliment, professor," she replied, gently mocking Alex's PhD.

Alex took in Jade's beauty for a moment that seemed to last minutes but was only fleeting. Jade had put just enough make-up on to accentuate her features and the effect was amazing. The car filled with the scent of her perfume and Alex got lost in the atmosphere. "So, are we going to eat?"

Jade asked, snapping Alex out of her trance.

"Sure." She fumbled for the gear stick.

Jade laughed and shook her head. Alex was not the most confident person when dealing with the relationship, she never had been. Although she had had many of them, they were mostly casual with only a couple lasting more than six months.

"Have you remembered to bring everything, professor?" Jade said, again having fun with her title.

"What title does a rock climbing architect use in their day-to-day life?" Alex teased Jade back for her previous comment.

"BOSS!" she replied. They both laughed.

The hotel sat at the north end of Ballachulish on the site of the original ferry crossing. It had been there for centuries and could now be accessed by the iron bridge that took all traffic heading north this far west. Alex had phoned to book the table for 7.30pm and they arrived with five minutes to spare.

On the drive up, Jade had been studying Alex with some amusement. She knew by now that she was interested in her and that the plan had worked. She'd always been confident in who and what she wanted, especially in relationships, and did not troll the local bars looking for a quick fling like some of the girls she knew.

They parked the pick-up and had a look at the menu in its neon-lit home on the outside wall of the main entrance, then went inside and made their way through to the restaurant. Alex caught the eye of the waiter and said she had a reservation for two at 7.30pm under the name McDonald. After exchanging pleasantries, the waiter gave them both a menu and took their drinks order, which fortunately for both was sparkling water. On returning with their water, the waiter asked if they were ready to order. Alex wanted the rib-eye with vegetables and potatoes, while Jade asked for the salmon with mixed vegetables.

After finishing dinner and refusing dessert, they paid the bill then headed to the decked area outside with their drinks where things were a bit quieter.

"I think the 'hidden' reference is to the Lost Valley and the middle part is about the watch, but who is the Gatekeeper?" Alex was pondering over the riddle when Jade spoke.

"Maybe the Gatekeeper isn't a who but a what?" Alex was puzzled. Jade continued, "You know the huge boulder at the start of the Lost Valley, did it not have an old name like 'the Sentry' or something like that? Maybe he's referring to that?"

"Do you know what, Jade, I think you may be right." They both sat beaming at each other.

"Now that's done, let's have a look at the blueprints and match them to this," Jade said, pulling an A4 sized sheet of paper from her bag.

"And what's that?" Alex asked.

"It's a schematic of a standard pocket watch that I printed off the internet. It should give us a rough comparison to the watch."

Sitting, Jade ran her trained eyes over both documents, scrutinizing every line. What she discovered was beyond them both. Alex's watch seemed to have many more inner workings to it than the one shown on the document. "Maybe it was just my grandfather's style to make it more detailed?" Alex theorized.

"Maybe," echoed Jade, "What if this is so complex because it has another purpose as it says in the riddle?" It was getting dark. Alex suggested they meet up again tomorrow and discuss it further.

"Why don't we climb up there at first light and get things rolling?" Jade replied. This took Alex by surprise, but she still found herself agreeing to the plan. With that, they spun round to Jade's home where she grabbed her climbing gear and extra equipment, clothes, and food. This all took her five minutes then she was back in the passenger seat.

"See, I told you it wouldn't take me long," she smiled, feeling incredibly pleased with herself. Alex just shook her head and laughed.

On entering the cottage, Alex apologized for the mess and tried to tidy up. Jade found the kettle and made some tea, letting her sort things out in the living room.

"Is it safe to come in?" she asked with a laugh.

"Er, think so." Alex threw the rest of her things into the small cupboard next to the kitchen. "You can see I wasn't expecting company," she said, getting the kitchen door for Jade.

"Not even me?" she said, a wry smile on her face. Leaving her to think about that, she sat the tea on the table.

"Um, nooo," Alex smiled. Jade grinned, then handed her a cup of tea.

"Don't you get lonely up here?" she asked.

"Sometimes solitude is the best medicine for the soul."

"What's the game plan for tomorrow then?" she asked, letting Alex take charge of the next day's adventure.

Alex thought for a second then grinned.

"Get up, get climbing!" Taking another sip of her tea, Jade nodded. Alex disappeared into the hall and returned with some blankets. She stood up to take them.

"No, guests get the bedroom, host gets the couch."

Jade put her arms around Alex's waist and whispered, "Alex, we are adults; we both know you are not spending the night on the couch." She kissed her softly on the neck, working her way up to her mouth. Alex responded in turn as they both got lost in each other's arms.

Jade led Alex to the bedroom, switching the light on then closing the door. They made love and spent the rest of the night lying together till morning.

Alex woke feeling a weight on her chest. Finally, being able to focus her vision, she could see it was Jade, her naked body gleaming in the early morning sunlight. Alex smiled up at her as Jade whispered to her.

"You'll die like your fucking kinsmen!"

Jade brought the large kitchen knife around from behind her back, clasping it in both hands as she drove the point towards Alex's heart.

Sitting bolt upright in bed with the remnants of her dream still in her head, Alex screamed, which brought Jade running from the kitchen. As she burst through the bedroom door, Alex recoiled in fear, still holding onto what remained of her nightmare.

"What is it?" Jade shouted.

Alex, who was still trying to get her bearings, told her.

"It was a nightmare, a horrible fucking nightmare." Her voice still quivered with fear.

After she'd calmed down, Alex told Jade about her dream. Jade was horrified, especially after the night they had spent together. Sitting on the bed she cradled Alex in her arms, telling her that no one would hurt her, not while she had breath in her body. Even at breakfast, Alex could still feel the knife as it touched her flesh. She half thought about calling off the day's expedition, but they desperately needed answers, now more than ever. Jade was a great comfort in the wake of the nightmare and had made breakfast and a strong coffee to help steady Alex's nerves. She had been both cause and cure to her present predicament.

After breakfast, they checked their gear and supplies then showered. Alex disappeared into the attic and returned with a long cloth bag. "Going fishing?" Jade asked.

"No," Alex replied, "Just being prepared." She pulled the katana samurai sword out of its bag.

"Are you some kind of ninja?" Jade frowned.

"No, but I've studied Kenjutsu up to fourth degree black belt."

"Well, Alex McDonald, we are full of surprises," Jade said, reaching for her backpack. Alex fetched her own, locking the sword in its bag before fastening it against the side. They jumped into the pick-up and headed for the glen.

It was a glorious day, the sun enhancing the different shades of green, grey, and purple that were in abundance in both the forest and mountainside. They talked throughout the short journey and agreed it would be good to park in the lower car park as it was the quietest and would use the walk to the bottom of the Lost Valley as a warm-up. Using the well-worn path that was deserted at this time in the morning, Jade and Alex picked up the pace trying to warm their muscles for the climb ahead.

The valley that lay between two of the Three Sisters was a popular tourist track but not for the fainthearted, especially in bad weather. Usually when climbing or walking in the mountains, it was customary to leave your chosen route with the hotel or mountain rescue, but on this day, they did neither because of the unusual circumstances of their quest. They chatted about their jobs, friends, and previous partners. It had been a while for both since they had got so physical that fast, but they agreed that there were no regrets. Taking the steep steps to the bridge that marked the start of the hike, they paused to take in the beauty of their surroundings. Looking over the rail into the crystal-clear water, they turned to one another and softly kissed, caressing each other as they did so. Alex broke her hold, smiling. "No time for fornication, there's a mountain to climb."

Jade laughed aloud, "Is that what I am to you, Alex McDonald? A loose woman?" Alex laughed and nodded her head as Jade slapped her hard on the butt, telling her, "That if she didn't get a move on, she'd have her wicked way with her." They both laughed.

"Promises, promises." Alex replied.

Chapter Twelve

They quickly reached the deer fence and climbed the eight-foot stile; from here on in, the terrain got noticeably steeper. Approaching the first gorge, Alex and Jade spoke very little, choosing to focus on their footing as it was very steep in sections, some one to two hundred feet in depth with sheer sides. If you fell there and lived, only a helicopter could get you out. Making their way up, they passed through an area with huge boulders that looked like they had been placed there by some giant hand, when in fact it was only the powerful force of erosion that had split them from the rock face with gravity doing the rest.

Now bathed in sunlight once again, they agreed to take a break at the ford in the river. Looking up from where they were, the rock face dominated on both sides with water rippling down, falling into the crystal stream below. There were so many different shades of green and brown, changing every time the sun disappeared behind a cloud. Many of the trees that survived up here were centuries old, their growth rate slowed by the harsh conditions, especially in winter.

Resting their bags against the rocks, they both pulled out some quick energy bars and ate them. Although they had water bottles, they chose to take a drink from the stream, the water cold and very refreshing. Unlike most other countries, it was possible to drink out of any Scottish mountain stream without fear of parasites or diseases. Looking at the ford in the stream, Alex thought of Dante's famous quote above the gates to the underworld; 'Abandon hope all ye who enter here!' Once they were on the other side, there was no turning back. Jade's voice brought her back to this world. "Earth calling Alex?" she inquired.

"Sorry, I was just thinking, are we sure we want to do this?" She replied.

"This is your adventure, not mine. I'm just the dimwitted sidekick that keeps the hero company." Her answer made Alex smile.

"Nice to see you know your place in the grand scheme of things."

"Cheeky bitch!" She covered the ground between them in a flash. "Ninja or no ninja, you're getting your sweet little ass kicked." Playfully, she punched Alex's arms then sat on her knee, cradling her face in her hands. She looked Alex in the eye.

"Alex, if anyone can figure this out, you can."

Alex pulled her closer, kissed her forehead and softly said, "Thanks. See, you're not that thick."

"Yooouuu," Jade laughed back at her.

Once across the ford, they made their way up the trail, the stream disappearing below on the right with a slab of flat rock meeting the main cliff face on the left. The path eased in angle as they reached the top and it lay there in front of them in all its beauty, the Lost Valley. They stood for a moment taking in the view all around them. The glen with its high cliffs, the snow still clinging to the rocks at the head of the valley, and the flat boulder-strewn floor with numerous colours of grass and high meadow flowers.

The Gatekeeper stood like an ancient sentinel, guarding the glen from all who ventured here. The path took them to the valley floor and a further fifty yards put them right against him.

"What do we do now, boss?" Jade's humour was never ending, thought Alex.

"I don't know, you're the brains of this outfit."

"Well, I'm glad you've finally recognized my genius, Professor McDonald."

Getting back to the business at hand, the pair looked for any signs on the rock, but they found none, except for one last part of it in shade that was covered in thick moss. They began feeling about in the rock; suddenly, Jade grabbed Alex by her jacket.

"There seems to be a void here!" She motioned with her left hand.

Alex followed her hand and sure enough, there was a circular hole in the rock about four feet off the ground, just the right size to fit her watch in. They cleaned it off and with the help of a small torch, they could see another smaller hole in the centre of the bigger one.

"What is it?" She looked at Alex.

"Beats me!" She replied.

"Well, you're a geologist, aren't you?" They laughed.

"Maybe it's some sort of ancient technology?" Alex offered and got her watch out.

She investigated the void then looked back at her watch. Reaching up, she placed it in the hole, but nothing happened. She took the watch back out, turned it around in her hand, then flipped the catch to release the back panel and looked inside. There seemed to be a corresponding hole exactly in the centre matching the one in the rock. Jade looked on. "Are you sure you want to do this?" Alex nodded her head.

"In for a penny!" Alex placed the watch in the hole with the front cover open. Nothing. Then a low mechanical hum like a drill sounded. As they looked at the face of the watch, the hands began to run backwards. They glanced at each other. Faster and faster the hands moved till they hit twelve o'clock, then everything went still. Alex felt a strange sensation pulling at her centre as the landscape around her started to distort and go out of focus.

"Alex!" Jade was screaming Alex's name as she reached

out to her.

Alex's hand caught Jade's arm as the world around them collapsed, different colours spiraling together, then total darkness.

Chapter Thirteen

Alex opened her eyes; she could still hear Jade calling her name. Looking to her right, she saw her off to one side, unconscious. Alex felt waves of nausea that finally made her throw up. Jade, now awake, wretched. "Jesus Christ, Alex, what was that and where are we?" She washed her mouth out with water from her bag then handed it to Alex.

They looked at their surroundings, which were very dimly lit. There was a roaring sound nearby, which they both thought must be a waterfall. Alex switched on her headtorch that she'd fished out of her bag. Stone walls surrounded them, they were in a cave which was spacious but showed signs of animal use. The beam of the head torch came across something metal; it was the watch. Alex eased it out of the wall and looked at the face, which still read midnight. Closing the front panel, she then retrieved the back cover from her pocket and clicked it back into place. "I'll check outside to get our bearings. You could have a root around in here, see if we can start a fire." Alex handed Jade the torch.

Alex was close to the waterfall when she saw the path that led out. On the other side of the waterfall, she found some driftwood washed up at the high-water mark. Hastily gathering enough wood to get things going, she headed back to the cave. Jade found her face with the beam. "Where's the fish and chips?" she teased her.

"You wish. In fact, you and me both," Alex replied.

They got the fire going with Alex's trusted spark stick. It seemed better to stay put till the next morning when the sun came up, if this place had a sun. Both had survival experience so knew how to ration their food and water. Tucking into their lavish meal of one square of chocolate, very extravagantly they each also had a nutrient bar and some water. After finishing, they got their bed rolls and sleeping bags out. Alex volunteered for wood collecting, given she'd already had her head torch on.

Sitting in the light of the fire, they were thinking of what options were available. Using the watch again seemed out of the question as it might put them in more peril. Not doing anything was out too, so it appeared logical to wait to see if there was a sunrise and investigate things further. Jade always found something funny to say at the right time and now was no different. "If this is your idea of a dirty night in, then I'm sadly underwhelmed," she quipped. Alex let out a huge belly laugh.

"Do you ever get depressed?"

"Not in the right company," Jade replied, snuggling up to Alex to kiss her. Jade's kiss was more out of comfort than passion; a cave in the middle of nowhere did not inspire lust.

Sunlight penetrated deep into the cave, instantly stirring them both from their dreams. Sitting, they watched the sunrise through the cascade of water and hugged each other in relief. Following the path that Alex had taken the previous night, they emerged into a glade, not unlike any you would find in the Highlands of Scotland. On returning to the cave, both carefully re-packed their backpacks leaving their temporary shelter as they had found it on arrival, apart from the vomit stains and fire embers. Climbing out of the glade, which sat higher than the surrounding area, there was nothing but trees as far as the eye could see. They headed in a northerly direction, assuming the sunrise was in the east. They saw familiar plants and insects while picking up a track through the forest. Alex had taken the sword from its pack and stowed it on the side of her bag, just in case.

The sun made the walk pleasant. Jade was telling Alex

about some of the so-called climbers she had had to deal with whilst working at the climbing centre. One guy, who was a risk to everyone including himself, was a rich kid who thought he could buy skill, but Jade had told him "The world don't work that way." He had lost it, threatening to have the centre closed on the grounds of malpractice. Alex shook her head and said she'd come across her fair share of assholes too, especially rich ones who thought they were not only above everyone but also that they could buy anything. "Money is all corrupting." Alex shook her head.

The sound of a horn split the peace in the forest. Jade and Alex froze in their tracks, trying to work out where the sound had come from and, more importantly, who had made it. They could hear voices in the distance but were unable to discern the dialect; it sounded vaguely Scandinavian. Hiding behind a tree, the voices were much closer now. A deer flew past the other side of their tree, startling them both. As they turned away, Alex could sense a presence close by. As they moved, they found themselves staring down at the tip of an arrow. Looking up, three to four men, tall with long hair, clothed in what looked like leather armor with Celtic style details worked into the hide. "Wait, wait, wait…" Alex shouted.

"Why are you talking in the common tongue? Where are you from?" The man with the bow replied. Jade noticed them looking at how both she and Alex were dressed.

"We came through a gate, behind a waterfall." The bowman released the tension in his weapon.

"We must take you to the elders, they have been waiting for you. Follow us. You may call me Kas." He asked them their names. Jade looked at Alex.

"This guy is two brain cells short of a Neanderthal."

"We're trying to make friends, not end up as dinner." Alex smiled.

Jade laughed out loud, bringing a scornful look from the rest of the strangers.

They entered the village, it seemed to be built into the forest itself. Dwellings were perched high and low with some at ground level. It was on this level that the main hall was situated and where they were heading for their meeting with the elders. The building seemed to rise from the very earth it sat in, thatched with grass that came down to the forest floor so that it blended seamlessly with its environment. There was a stone and wood facade with wooden uprights carved with mystical beasts, as were the large wooden doors at the entrance to the hall. Kas opened a door; he motioned Alex inside but blocked Jade. "You stay outside," he said, staring straight at her with cold blue eyes.

"I'll be here if you need me." Jade said to Alex.

Entering the hall, Kas put his shoulder against the great door. It gave with a massive sigh like a cry from one of the mystical beasts carved into the wood. Inside there were large wooden columns that supported the roof and a central hole that let the smoke out but gave little illumination. The hall was lit by a series of torches that sat in iron holders on each of the main beams, and the air had a misty blue haze to it coming from the embers in the fire. Alex could see a group of four men sitting at a table. There were two younger men sat back at either side of the room and both had swords; guards, she thought.

As they came closer, Kas announced to the group, "These are the ones who came through the gate, another waits outside."

The old men studied Alex. They were all dressed roughly the same as the other warriors in armour. One had tattoos on one side of his face and it was he who spoke first. "Speak!" the tattooed man said. Alex looked perplexed.

"I don't know what you want to hear?"

"Your voice will do fine." This brought a ripple of laughter from the old man's cohorts. Alex was the only one who wasn't laughing. The old man spoke again.

"You're a McDonald, then?"

Hearing her name caught Alex off guard, bringing more laughter from the small congregation. The old man spoke again, leaving Alex to gather her thoughts. "I knew your grandfather, James McDonald. He told me this day would come." He looked at the charm around Alex's neck and continued. "The amulet you bear is from the blackest of times in our history, a time when man was weak. Power is an all-conquering force."

Finding her voice, Alex asked, "How do know my name?"

"You are not the first to walk this path nor to hold the knowledge of the other realms. You are, however, the first to wear that amulet in this realm for a long time. It has been locked in the mountains for millennia under the watchful eye of your clan. Your bloodline being the only warriors able enough to hold the darkness at bay, you and you alone hold the fate of all the realms in your hands." During this time, the old man's eyes never left Alex's.

Finally, after what seemed like an age, she spoke. "I'm a scientist, not a warrior. I never knew anything about this until last week. It can't be true. My grandfather was a watchmaker, not a soldier, he…"

The old man stood up and came around the table, taking Alex by the shoulders.

"Your kin have sacrificed more than you'll ever know and that includes your grandfather and your father. If indeed you are a scientist, why do you carry a sword?"

It couldn't be true, could it? Alex was thinking back to all the training in the mountains and in the dojo. She thought about her grandfather and grandmother and all the sacrifices they had made for her to be the woman she was now. Then there was Jade; could she let this 'darkness' take away the world that was their home? She turned to the old man.

"What do you need me to do?"

Whilst Alex was in the hall, Jade, much to her annoyance, sat outside gathering inquisitive looks from the villagers. Feeling restless and not knowing how long their meeting was going to be, she thought it would be a good idea to get familiar with her surroundings. There were pleasant smiles from some and scornful looks from others, mainly the hunters. 'Boys only club, some things never change,' she thought to herself. She took off her bag and retrieved some chocolate from it. While doing so, she caught the attention of a young boy, no more than five years old, she guessed. Unwrapping the sweet then snapping off a couple of squares, Jade held them out to the boy, who didn't move. She took a piece off what remained of the bar and popped it in her mouth, making a yummy sound as she ate. The boy by this time was sold on the fact that whatever the strange woman had, it wasn't poisonous, and sounded too delicious not to eat. With all that thought, he cautiously approached Jade. Just as he reached out his hand to take the treat, one of the hunters slapped it out of her hand. She reeled on him. "What's your problem? It's only fucking chocolate!" As she said this, Jade noticed the man's nearest hand had been pulled back ready to be released in her direction.

Just as he was about to slap her, they heard the old man's voice.

"Asdrin, she is our guest, show her some respect!" His words were spoken softly but with an obvious authority. The hunter apologized and bowed his head.

Crossing the clearing, Alex asked if Jade was okay. She glared at the hunter then turned to introduce Jade to the old man she now knew as Gorran. After being introduced to Gorran, Jade and Alex were shown to a small dwelling that was unused and was for now their home from home. The chief had told the village that the visitors were to be treated as honoured guests and should be shown their best hospitality.

Their new home was built around a sturdy oak type tree, basically a treehouse, with a small spiral staircase to the living level. Like the other structures in the village, the main construction components including the doors and beams were elaborately carved with a mixture of beasts of lore and delicate vines and leaves.

Alex filled Jade in on the events of the great hall. As usual, Jade took it all in her stride. There was a knock on the door. Alex opened it and Kas stood there with something over his arm. He apologized to them both for his behaviour earlier and handed them some clothes to change into. "You will need these to blend in," he told them.

As Kas turned to leave, Alex caught his arm. "Thank you, I think this is difficult for all involved." The warrior nodded and bid them farewell.

"Nice off-the-shoulder little number, what do you think?" Jade said, slipping into her new clothes, which just about fitted her. Alex gave a little wolf whistle and finished getting into hers. "Well, whatcha think?"

"Very fetching," she replied.

Alex was dressed like the men with a leather breastplate, a dragon scale design around her mid-section. On her legs she wore soft hide leggings that were braided up the outside with leather laces and simple boots on her feet. Jade had leggings, a full-length skirt with boots and a long-sleeved linen top under a leather bodice.

The room was simple, a bed, a fireplace with a stone hearth, some shelves, and a large box, not unlike Alex's grandfathers. This was where they put their clothes and backpacks. There were a couple of wicker-backed chairs with various candles sprinkled around the interior and a table with some fresh bread, cheese and a flagon of milk. "Housewarming gift?" Alex quipped.

There was a bowl and a large bucket of water for washing.

Making light of things, Jade asked Alex.

"Is this an ex-show home? It seems to have all the mod-cons, that is, except a loo." Alex laughed.

"I think the loo is outside. I mean quite literally outside. Remember to whistle when you're in the bushes." They both laughed and lay down on the bed. Looking up, they could see the elaborate mix of wood and thatch that made up the roof. With that, they both fell asleep.

The following day, they rose to a knock at the door. Getting up, Alex opened it and was greeted by Kas. "My father has prepared a feast in your honour and bids you to come and eat with us."

"We'd be honoured. I wasn't aware that Gorran was your father?"

"You didn't need to know at the time." The warrior tipped his head in a shallow bow and headed in the direction of the great hall.

Jade was up now and had washed some of the sleep from her face. She turned to Alex.

"This will be our first function as a couple, are you excited?" Teasing Alex was becoming a hobby.

"I say, Lady Keegan, it would be my very great pleasure if you would accompany me to the ball!" She raised her elbow for Jade to take.

"Well, Lady McDonald, that is such a kind offer, who could refuse?" Jade took her arm and they kept up the pretense till they got to the door. Alex opened it, bowing.

"Ma'am."

"Why thank you."

They turned around and noticed that a couple of the villagers had watched the end of their short play. Alex and Jade immediately dropped out of character and smiled, then rushed across the courtyard to the hall.

Approaching the great building, they could hear talking and laughter. The massive door was lying open and on walking through, Gorran shouted Alex's name, rising to greet them but stopping as if he'd been held by some unseen hand. The old man's eyes were locked on Jade. Finally released from his trance, Gorran came around the table and took Jade's hand. He spoke softly to her. "Dear girl, it's as if my daughter has come back to me from the afterlife. This is one of her dresses you are wearing."

Jade could not take her eyes from the old man. She had seen the mixture of sadness and joy he had on seeing the dress being worn again. "Thank you so much for the dress, it is so beautiful," she smiled and squeezed his hands with a soft love that a daughter would feel for their father. He returned the smile.

There were various plates of game from birds to hare, with the centre piece being a boar of some kind. Also on the table were vegetables, bread, butter, and some fruit. This was an existence diet for a people who worked and foraged the land to survive. As they spoke to the old man, it became clear that his people had a long lineage going back to the times of a race called the Elves. They were known as the Veldan; in the old tongue, it meant 'People of the Trees'. Gorran explained to them that some of the realms were like theirs and that others could be quite different.

The food was well prepared and delicious. As they ate, some of the others at the table took it in turns to sing. Alex and Jade could only listen to the flow of the music as it was being sung in the native tongue, but even so, it did create a pleasant atmosphere. Kas turned to both Alex and Jade. "Sing us a song of your world."

They looked at each other, then at their hosts. It became apparent that there was no backing out. Alex was frantically trying to come up with a song when Jade said, "What about Dumbarton's Drums?" Alex shrugged her shoulders.

"Fine with me."

The song was about love, and they sang it as a duet. What surprised them both was how good it sounded. When they finished, everyone in the great hall applauded.

When the applause died down, Gorran, Kas, Asdrin, Alex and Jade moved away from the main body of villagers who were still singing and celebrating. The chief motioned for everyone to take a seat, which they all did. "Now to the reason you are here, my friends." Again, his eyes were drawn to Alex's charm. "These amulets of power have cursed the realms for millennia. The Dark One knows that you hold the key to the destruction of these bringers of death. There are other amulets in the realms that you must retrieve. Most will be given up willingly, others will take skillful negotiations, and I have asked Kas and Asdrin to be your guides through the other lands." Alex knew there was no point in protesting. She somehow understood that this was the right thing to do, or that's what her intuition was saying to her. She looked into the old man's eyes.

"When do we leave?"

Gorran smiled, "Tomorrow."

Everyone at the table was now focused on the plan, which was to travel light, gathering resources as they went and rendezvousing with those who were sympathetic to their cause. As Alex and Jade stood to leave, Kas gave them a torch. "Keep the fire alive and a candle burning at night. There are things that exist in the darkness. Do not let them into your minds."

"I know and thank you." Both parties nodded and went their separate ways.

Jade never questioned Alex's decision; she knew it was the right thing for them to do. They walked back to their dwelling. "Do you think that the dreams you've been having are part of this bigger picture?"

"Yes, definitely," Alex replied, but she wasn't smiling, adding more worry to what Jade was already carrying.

Alex awoke, the fire was dead and there was no light in the room. She could feel Jade was tense, so gently squeezed her arm then whispered. "I'll try to get an ember from the fire and light a candle." Jade said nothing.

There was an air of dread in the room. Something malevolent lurked in the dark. Alex moved towards the fire in smooth strides, her eyes becoming accustomed to the gloom inside the room. She became aware of a pressure around her throat. Reaching up, she found a pair of hands – they were Jade's.

Kas had heard a woman's voice and knew immediately that it was Jade's. He leaped out of bed, stopping only to cover his modesty, grabbing a torch and his sword before bolting for the door, which rattled on its hinges as he sped outside. The scene that greeted Kas as he burst through the door of his guests would stay with him for days. He entered and brought the torch forward to see clearer. Jade was on top of a now unconscious Alex's hands around her throat. It was the look on her face that so disturbed Kas. Jade was foaming at the mouth and her eyes were rolled back leaving only the whites showing. She was talking in a low guttural voice that sounded like, "Maza craza da, maza craza da…" Kas knew that this was dark magic.

He snatched the amulet from around his neck and pressed it against Jade's forehead. On contact with the metal, her limp form flew backwards and hit the wall next to the bed. "Be gone, foul beast, from the pit. Leave these souls in peace for they shall not be vessels for your black deeds. Be gone…"

Alex was coming round and could hear Kas' words. Looking up at Kas, she asked with a rasp in her voice, "What happened… where is Ja…" Alex passed out.

Chapter Fourteen

Tom was pacing the room again. Now and then, he would catch a glimpse of himself reflected in the windows, his hair matted with a thick growth of stubble that would shortly be a full-blown beard. Like him, his room was a disheveled mess; this was a far cry from the young eager scientist of a few years ago. He always found that the path to doing good work was taking control of one's personal life, especially in keeping his immediate surroundings and himself neat, tidy and in order. These changes had not gone unnoticed by the director of CERN, Professor Paul Grearson, who had arranged a meeting with Tom that afternoon. This was the reason for Tom's agitation. "What the fuck has my appearance got to do with my work?" Tom shouted this at the walls of the room, getting no response.

His waking hours were becoming as confused as his nights, where the lines between both were beginning to blur. In fact, the two were merging into one big cycle of fear, frustration, and anger. Looking at his watch, he could see that it was nearly time for his meeting with, as Tom called him, 'the idiot Grearson'.

"Hi Tom, come in, take a seat please." The director of the facility spoke in a neutral tone and guided Tom to the chair straight across from where he was sitting.

Grearson was a career scientist with a background in physics and mathematics. The director had ended up in his current role by means of his uncanny ability to get the job done and having a calm authority that he wore like a second skin. At the age of sixty with salt and pepper hair, Paul kept reasonably fit, maintaining the features and physique of a man ten years younger, which in his present job was a big bonus. Right now, he was dealing with a colleague who by all intents and purposes was in the middle of some personal crisis. "Tom, do you understand why I've asked for this meeting today?" Paul had now shifted his tone to a softer engaging level to try and ease his colleague's obvious anxiety.

Tom thought for a second then replied. "Not really, but I'm sure you're going to clarify things for me." There was an edge of sarcasm in his tone, which Paul didn't rise too. The director chose his next sentence very carefully.

"Tom, it's come to my attention that you seem to have been under a bit of pressure over the last few weeks and as a colleague, I was wondering if there was anything that I could do for you or if you needed to talk about something? To get it off your chest, say? I'm here as a fellow scientist to help you."

The director's offer caught Tom off guard; he seemed genuinely concerned. Tom couldn't see any reason why he needed to talk to his boss about anything. There was no way he could tell Paul about his plans or what they were about. When he finally spoke, his voice had lost its edge. "Well, it's just the workload of teaching and running my personal stuff in the background, you know how things can cross over." Tom was staring at the table then looked up at his boss.

Paul pushed forward with his agenda. "Funny you should say that Tom because we've all been there once or twice in our own journeys, me included. It's my responsibility to notice when these situations are coming to the surface and to take positive action for the benefit of all."

Tom had a sinking feeling in the pit of his stomach. His boss had put him in a corner, and he was desperately trying to think of a way out of this trap. He had given his director all the ammunition needed. Trying frantically to regain control and failing, the professor asked for his teaching schedule to be reduced; at that, the trap snapped shut. Paul looked Tom square in the eye. "You need some time off. I've rescheduled your time on the collider and given it to the visiting group of grad students from MIT. Your spot will come in behind these guys roughly a week after your original time. I think you should take this break to reflect on what has happened recently." Tom was on his feet before the director had finished speaking.

"You can't do this to me. I know things have gotten slightly out of hand recently, but I will get my shit together. I NEED THE TIME ON THE COLLIDOR!"

Grearson was slightly taken aback by the venom in the professor's words but, as usual, he kept his cool and stood his ground. "I'm sorry, Tom, but I've made my decision, a decision that is for the benefit of all and not solely directed at you. Take the time to reevaluate what is important to you, your job, or your personal goals as a scientist." As the director said this, his eyes never left his colleague's glare.

Tom was furious but he knew if he made a scene, it would be the end of his career at the facility. He sat back down and gathered himself.

"Maybe you're right, Paul. I've put so much work in over the last while and it's just got on top of me. I think the rest will do me good," he lied, "and I'll return fresh and more focused on my job and studies." Tom begrudgingly shook the director's hand, turned to leave, but Paul kept his grip.

"Tom, you're a brilliant scientist and an asset to our work here, we need you in good shape to get the best out of you."

His parting words brought no comfort to Tom, who was already thinking about what his other darker boss might do to him.

Chapter Fifteen

Jade woke in a daze with no memory of the previous night's events. "Where's Alex?" she cried.

Kas reassured her. "She's fine, my father is speaking with him just now." Jade sat up in bed, waves of pain coursed through her body.

"What the hell happened to me? I feel like I've been in some kind of accident." When Kas finally spoke, it brought chills to every part of her being.

"You were possessed by a demon sent by the darkness to kill both you and Alex." Kas was looking directly into Jade's eyes; she could see he wasn't lying. "This may be hard for you to hear but I must tell you."

"Tell me what?" Jade replied. Kas was quiet for a moment.

"You tried to kill Alex. Rather, the demon possessing you did." Jade was numb. She struggled to hold back the tears that were welling up in the corners of her eyes.

"How could this happen? I mean, why?" Kas went on to tell her that there were black forces aligned with the Darkness that would carry out his will in all the realms.

"Maza craza da or Marsan Crissdan." Gorran was trying to decipher the chant that Kas had heard the night before. He told Alex that the words had been spoken in an old tongue that not many living still knew, but Gorran's father and he were direct descendants of one of these ancient people.

"One of the fables from this time was of a black witch called Marsan Crissdan who fed off the souls of mortals and could possess anyone she chose. Some women used the name to put fear in their children or to keep them out of places they should not be. Lore has it that she was destroyed by a powerful wizard and thrown into the depths." Gorran had been speaking in a soft tone, as if the person in question was sitting in the room.

The old man continued to speak to Alex, telling her that his ancestors were healers and knew how to use magic to protect and cure. "The thing that saved both you and Jade was Kas', the talisman he wears around his neck. It is made of silver with a spirit stone at its centre. It has immensely powerful magic that will only work if the person's heart is pure."

Gorran instructed Alex that they must continue their journey within two days. The old man had felt a shift in the realm and knew it was time to put the plan into action. He took out a small box, taking a key off his neck which he slid into the lock. With a smooth click, the locking mechanism deactivated, and the lid lifted to reveal a small silk-like purse. On opening the bag, Gorran told Alex that he'd been waiting for some time to give the charm to its guardian. He placed it in Alex's hand. "Now that you're here, I can pass it to you." Gorran warned Alex to conceal both amulets till the time came to give them back to the stars. The old man said no more on the subject.

Alex walked through the door; Jade lay awake. Kas had been watching over her in his absence but now bid them good day and left, closing the door behind him. Jade stretched her arms out to Alex, beckoning for her embrace. She lay on the bed and took her in her arms. "I'm sorry, I'm so sorry!" Jade whispered to her. Alex kissed the top of her head, "There's nothing to be sorry for." They lay for a long time just enjoying the feel of each other's touch.

"We're leaving soon, maybe tomorrow, if you're strong enough?" Jade looked at Alex.

"Do we have any other choice?" she asked her. Alex gazed

into Jade's eyes.

"Staying will put the village and all the people in danger. If we keep moving, we're a harder target to attack." Jade sighed, nodded her head in agreement.

That night, they ate and slept under the roof of their host and there were no more visitors. In the morning, Jade woke still wrapped in Alex's arms. She lay a little while enjoying the secure feeling that she gave her, then kissed her on each eyelid, Alex started to stir. Jade got out of bed and went to the small table; she washed her face then patted it dry with a hand towel. By the time she had done this, Alex was awake and dressed. She came to Jade, grabbing her roughly. "Wench, where's my breakfast?" She wrapped her arms around Jade's neck.

"Your food is in the kitchen, ma'am. Do you want me to fetch it?"

Pulling her close, Alex said, "I have all that I need right here." She kissed Jade. They held each other's embrace for a while till it was broken by a knock at the door. On opening it, Alex could see it was Kas.

"Will you eat with us?" he asked. Alex nodded.

After eating breakfast, Alex and Jade met with Gorran, who was giving a pep talk to the rest of their little expeditionary force. The old man put his arm around the shoulders of first Alex then Jade. "I have not known you very long, but I feel as if you are my own kin. It is with a heavy heart that I must send you on this journey, but send you I must, for the benefit of all." There was a profound honesty in Gorran's words, and it touched them very deeply. "My sons will be both your guides and protectors on this journey. I'm not going to tell you it will be easy, far from it. There are many dangers out there so you must listen to Kas and Asdrin, take their counsel when needed. May all that is good in our realms protect you and bring you back safely, my dearest friends!" Jade took Gorran's hands in hers and planted a kiss on both of his cheeks, then hugged him as if it were her own father.

"My only wish is to return here," she told him, "To see you again and visit this enchanted place without the shadow of darkness hanging over us. You have shown hospitality knowing you would be in the line of danger, but still you took us in. I thank you for Kas, without whom we would surely be dead, and I thank your beautiful daughter for the clothes I stand in, wishing only that I do her justice on the path ahead." Gorran took Jade in his arms and whispered so only she could hear.

"My daughter is alive. You and she are of the one spirit." He kissed her on the cheek, losing the battle with his tears as they rolled down his face and dropped to the ground. Quickly wiping his face and cursing the cold air for watering his eyes, Gorran turned to Alex. "You have a warrior's heart, that I know. You must keep your wits sharp, as sharp as that blade you carry. Cold steel is the only language some people understand. You have been chosen for a task most would run in fear from. I bless you and the rest of this group. May your travels be swift and the nights peaceful till next you find your way back to us."

Alex took Gorran by the forearms as was custom. Staring into the old man's eyes, she said, "I can see why my grandfather liked you, you remind me of him in so many ways. You have given me a responsibility, a task that I shall not shy from. I will lay down my life for a cause that is just. We will return when there will be tales of enemies vanquished and wrongs put right. This I promise you, Gorran, son of Thern." The chief beamed, knowing Kas had instructed Alex on a warrior's proper farewell.

Kas took Alex and Jade to the edge of the village where they met with Asdrin. There was a small pack for each of them containing some food, herbs, and extra provisions; they were travelling light. As Asdrin handed them their packs, Kas disappeared for a moment and returned with a dog. 'Dog' was a bit of a general description; it was mostly wolf-like with a cross of some kind, which at this point Alex and Jade were too stunned to work out.

Kas asked Alex then Jade to come and introduce themselves to the dog, whose name was Faldor or, to give him his full name, Faldor the Throat Ripper. This name brought no comfort to either of them. Jade went first, moving smoothly up to the beast with her hand out in front. The great dog could smell her scent and as his nose connected with her skin, it was instantly transferred to its internal memory. Next was Alex, who repeated the process that Jade had performed then reached her hand out to stroke the beast's head. Her hand froze in mid-air as Faldor emitted a low growl while lifting the corner of his mouth. "He becomes your friend in his own time." Kas laughed.

The expedition was gathered. They did a final check that they had everything. Alex took her spark stick, sword, and nothing else, not wanting to be found with strange devices from her realm. The rest she left in the village under the watchful eye of Gorran.

Kas turned to Alex and asked, "Do you know how to use that?" dropping his eyes to the katana. Alex picked an apple from her bag then gave herself some room. She then tossed the apple in the air and thumbed the guard with her right hand to release the steel from its scabbard. With a smooth action, she drew the sword free, cutting the descending apple cleanly in half, returning the blade before the fruit hit the ground.

"Does that answer your question?" she asked. Both Kas

and Asdrin had never seen such speed in a blade.

"You have some skill with your sword, but have you ever killed anyone with it?" Alex measured his response.

"Not yet, but the day is still early!" At that, the warriors started laughing.

"You have a good sense of humor, Alex. It will help on this journey." Kas, still smiling, turned to Jade. He reached into his belt, brought out a small knife and handed it to her. She thanked him and asked him for a bow.

"A bow is a man's weapon!" he snarled.

Jade took the bow and pointed at a knot in a tree about a hundred yards away.

"See that knot?" Kas nodded. Knocking her arrow, she pulled back on the sinuous string and took aim. There was a soft twang as the arrow left the bow. Watching with awe, Kas couldn't believe his eyes when the arrow hit its mark. The warrior turned to Jade; his next words stunned her.

"I have spoken ill of you, Jade, please forgive me for my arrogant thoughts." Waving her hand telling him there was no need to apologize, she went to hand the weapon back. Kas held up his hand.

"Your skill outweighs mine. Keep the bow, it is now in the hands of its rightful owner." He bowed his head. She thanked him for his gift.

"Does the bow have a name?" she inquired.

"You are the owner now; it is your choice to name the weapon."

"I think I'll call it True Heart; may it find the centre of any untrue spirit that comes our way." Kas smiled.

"You have surprised me today. I am now more hopeful for our quest." After he spoke, they laughed and took the path north.

Leaving the forest behind, they passed into a vast grass savanna with the odd tree thrown in for good measure. Alex noticed that the conversation had gone quiet on entering the grassland; even Jade did not speak.

"Hey, what's with the silence?" Alex quizzed Jade. She shushed her.

"Do you ever watch natural history programs? Big things eat smaller things on the plains."

"Well thank you for reassuring me. I was only mildly scared, now I'm scared," she said jokingly. Kas stopped and Asdrin motioned for Alex to be quiet.

"What's up?" Jade asked in a whispered voice.

"Faldor has the scent of something and depending on his reaction, we will either eat it or run in the opposite direction, fast."

The dog began running followed by the rest of the group. They had chosen their response well; the beast that was on their tracks had a good nose but poor vision. It was a type of monstrous badger, roughly about the same size as a lion. Usually, they could be found hunting at dusk, unless they were old or injured. The group thought it must have been old as it gave up its pursuit relatively quickly.

The Veldan called these plains 'The Lands of Death'. Being mostly forest dwellers where there was always somewhere to take cover if needed, out here there was little to none. It would be a full day walking to cross the savanna to reach the North Wood and the realm gate that lay beyond that.

They were about halfway across when they were attacked again, this time by a more cunning foe. Once more, it was Faldor who first sensed the great beast. It was close to them but downwind; the only reason the dog got its scent was by a passing whirlwind. Kas had seen the dog's reaction and whispered softly to the others. "We may be in trouble. Do

not change your stride or look around, we are being stalked!"
Jade and Alex looked at each other, then copied the warriors
as they drew their weapons.

Alex was looking down trying to make her posture as
non-threatening as possible when she noticed that the grass
was bone dry as it crunched under her feet. Alex spoke to the
others as they walked; all were nodding in agreement with
her plan. As the group walked forward, they began to take
handfuls of dead grass, which was about three foot long, fold
it in the middle then twist it at the bottom. Once they had
enough grass, Alex took out her spark stick, and they began
lighting their torches. As they did this, the great beast made
its move, but they managed to catch it off guard as in unison
they raised their torches to keep the monster at bay. It worked
for a moment.

Alex had never seen such a beast; it had a skin tone like
a lion with a series of faded dark stripes like a tiger, perfect
camouflage for this environment. The head was altogether
more interesting with two pairs of eyes, one set on the front
of the head and the others at the same level on the sides. Its
teeth were immense with huge upper and lower canines, like a
sabretooth on steroids. The beast was prowling back and forth
looking for a weak spot but there were none. Alex called out
to the others. "We need to burn the grass in a large arc around
this thing, so it thinks there's no way through. Downside is
that when we set the grass on fire, the wind is against us and
will fan the flames in our direction."

"I'd rather burn than be eaten by this thing," Kas shouted
to Alex.

They spread out and the beast ran from one to the other
trying to paw through at them, but the fear of fire kept it at
bay. As the fire got bigger and formed a large arc, they kept
hold of their torches and ran. Fed by its own heat, the fire

grew in intensity, threatening to overrun them. In the distance they could still hear the great beast's roar in the background. Finding the edge of the burn line, they kept running for a few miles before finally stopping when they came across a rock-strewn island offering them shelter and a well-earned rest.

"What was that thing?" Alex asked, "Looked like something straight out of a nightmare."

"It's a Venk or Silent Death. We're lucky to be alive," Kas replied, "It probably came across Faldor's scent then ours and homed in on it." His look was so intense and brought no comfort to Jade.

Deciding to make camp for the night, they found a cave recessed deep in the rock that just about fitted them all. They gathered dead wood from the few trees that grew in their sanctuary, enough to do them till morning. After the day's exertions, the group took turns to sleep and stand guard till dawn rose and gave birth to a new day.

Something was wrong. That was what Faldor's body language told everyone as they wondered what fate awaited them outside. The Venk circled the island of rock, thick globules of saliva dripping from its massive lower jaw. Inside the cave Kas was formulating an escape plan. He knew that the beast was a visual hunter and that the best way of incapacitating it would be to impair its vision. Kas turned to Jade. "Have you ever killed with a bow?" he asked.

Their plan was for Jade to shoot the Venk in one of its forward-facing eyes and one of the side-facing ones. They surmised it should stop the beast from being able to position itself to attack them. "Are you ok to do this?" She thought for a moment.

"Normally I shoot targets or for food. I've never had to shoot anything to save my life, let alone anyone else's." Asdrin hadn't said a lot on the journey, just made conversation, but now he spoke.

"There is nothing wrong with taking a life to save yourself or others, as long as you show proper respect to the thing you kill." Jade inquired as to what he meant. Asdrin said it was their custom to honour the dead, be they an enemy, a loved one or an animal. They all demanded one's respect at the end. She had never seen Asdrin in this light before and it changed her perception of him. He spoke about the fact that Faldor was a sacred animal to them, often seen as a returned loved one who had come back to be a part of their world again. Jade told them that it had been the same in her realm in the past. A tribe called the Celts held horses in high regard, as well as other religions that had many sacred animals such as cows, elephants and even snakes. Each time she spoke of a different animal, Jade gave a brief description of the beast. Some sounded fantastical to the warriors while others they said existed in their realm but had a different name.

The conversation had taken them away from the matter at hand. Time was of the essence, so Jade picked up her bow and tied her quiver to the waistband of the bodice she wore. Kas had agreed to use Faldor as a decoy to maneuver the beast, which would hopefully give her enough time to hit the targets. They heard the Venk move off; it was getting into a pattern in its pacing, so they waited till it was at its farthest point to their left, which would give a good vantage point to shoot from the right. They all eased themselves from the cave then climbed the massive boulders that acted as their barricade.

On reaching the top, they peered out to get a look at the beast. It had turned and was heading back. Jade crawled over the edge of the uppermost rock to sight her target. Tracking its line, she pulled on the bow, her body trembling with fear. She changed her breathing, finding a rhythm to steady her arm.

Seeing a spot just ahead of its front right eye, she let out half a breath and at the same time released the arrow from her grip.

The Venk roared as the arrow hit home, immediately snapping the shaft to rid itself of the pain. It rolled about on the ground for some time before getting back to its feet, resigned to the injury to its eye. Faldor moved out to the left, leaping from rock to rock with consummate ease. The wounded beast tracked the dog's movement thinking it had an easy meal when an immense pain ripped through the right of its head, again snapping the shaft of the arrow as it writhed in agony.

As it stood up, it could not focus its vision properly as opposite sides of its optic nerve had been irreparably damaged. It saw movement and could sense something approaching from the front, lashing out wildly. Asdrin and Alex had positioned themselves before the beast, leaving Kas with a chance to flank it coming up from its right-hand side. His sword drawn, he plunged it deep into the base of its skull, severing the spinal column. The Venk writhed for a while due to the massive trauma to its nervous system. The warriors dropped to one knee and bowed their heads to show a mark of respect. They cut out the beast's heart, wrapped it in cloth and placed it in Asdrin's shoulder bag. Kas turned to Jade and when he spoke it was with great pride. "You have a warrior's spirit. You stood your ground against a larger foe." He bowed his head in respect of her valor.

Kas then addressed the whole group. "This mighty foe has passed to the other side. May the Great Spirit let him return in human form to fight alongside us in times to come." Once again, they bowed their heads.

They buried the great beast's carcass in the earth and covered the spot with rocks. Alex held Jade tightly, knowing how much courage it had taken her both physically and mentally to shoot the beast.

At the edge of the North Wood, they all felt relieved to have some permanent cover. Alex and Kas cleared a sight for camping while Jade and Asdrin collected the all-important wood stock for the night's fire. Asdrin found some edible mushrooms that they could have with their meal later and showed Jade some of the plants that were herbs, fruits, and berries. Kas had asked Alex to show him how to use the spark stick as he had been using his drill stick, which was good but took too much time and energy. Kas sat by the fire with an incredibly pleased look on his face; his lesson had gone well.

Asdrin had set up a tripod to hang their small cooking pot that had been filled with water from a nearby stream. Now that the pot was boiling, they unwrapped the Venk's heart, set it inside, then left the organ to cook. Kas had told Alex and Jade it was an old and sacred tradition to eat the heart of a slain beast, but both were a little uneasy about eating the meat of the monster that had wanted to kill them. That said, if it needed to be done, they would not be rude and refuse. Once the meat was nearly cooked, Asdrin added a few herbs and the mushrooms. The group exchanged stories while they waited for their feast. Alex told the warriors about her job as a geologist; they laughed and laughed, then apologized for being so rude. "We all have work in the great way of things. In your world, these things have an importance." Alex accepted their apology.

"Yes, my job is important, but I agree it does get very boring at times, unless I'm studying volcanoes, then it gets a bit hairy."

"What's a volcano?" Kas asked.

"It's like a mountain on fire with rivers of fire running…" Asdrin stood up quickly.

"You study fire mountains?"

"Yes," Alex replied calmly.

"Well, my friend, you are a braver warrior than us. If we see a fire mountain, we usually run." Alex laughed, then everyone joined in; the mood around the fire was a happy one.

Sitting together, they all forgot there was still the rest of the North Wood to travel. It was a perilous journey that the warriors had kept from their companions, not wanting to put fear into their hearts. Just to be safe, they agreed to have a guard rotation so all could rest from the day's exertions. Alex was on the last watch, taking over from Asdrin. She sat listening to the night, some familiar sounds and some not so.

The beast came in slowly, with stealth, taking Kas first in its powerful jaws. His gurgling screams woke the others, but it was too late. As the Venk rounded on Asdrin, a powerful blow sliced through his mid-section, spilling his intestines onto the fire. Jade was screaming his name then her voice fell silent, the darkness sparing Alex the scene of utter carnage that Jade had suffered. There was a foul breath clawing at her throat. Alex tried to scream her name into the night but not one sound could be heard coming from her lips. Then came the voice, soft at first but growing in intensity. "Go back, Alex, go back. GO BACK NOW OR YOU WILL BRING DEATH TO ALL OF THEM. Go back, go back…"

"Alex, Alex, Alex…" As she opened his eyes, she could see Kas' face, his strong hands shaking her by the shoulders. Alex broke free, scrambling backwards across the ground on her hands, propelled by her feet which were sliding in the dirt.

"No, no, no, you're all dead, the Venk… and Jade is gone, oh my God, she's gone!" There was a soft voice calling his name.

"Alex, Alex my love, it's me. You were attacked again, like you were back in the cottage." Alex could hardly see Jade's face through the tears but when she took her hand, Alex knew it was her and that she was alive. Jade pulled her close, Alex openly sobbing as she cradled her in her arms.

Alex told the others of her terror. They all could sympathize with her outpouring of emotion. Kas told Alex that the darkness would use anything to control a situation to its advantage, even using a threat to the love of friends and family in manipulating the mind of its victims to gain an advantage.

Asdrin and Kas went to gather some wood and herbs to make a soothing tea, as well as to give Alex and Jade some time together. Jade held Alex's face in her hands then leaned in to tenderly kiss her.

"You're safe now and I will not let anything hurt you." They held each other closely for a moment.

"It was so real," Alex said in a soft voice, "I could feel everything, smell the death on its breath and hear that bastard in my head and the things he said..." Her voice tailed off. When Alex spoke again, she was looking at Jade straight in the eye.

"Then there was... I thought I'd lost you; it was a feeling I couldn't bear. You have become such a big part of my life in such a short time and..." Jade put her index finger on her lips.

"I know, you have been here in my heart for many years. Finally we're together, saving the world and being chased by monsters. You know how to impress a girl, I'll give you that, my love. I held back on giving my heart to anyone, then you came along and the walls I'd put up came tumbling down, for you." Tears were running down her face. Alex cradled Jade's face in her hands and wiped her tears away.

"I never knew you felt this way. I'm a bit like you, no one has ever gotten this close until now. You mean the world to me, my love, and no matter what happens I want you to know that Ok?" They kissed each other passionately then parted as Kas and Asdrin returned.

"Hope we're not disturbing anything?" Kas announced on

entering. The two lovers just looked at each other then laughed.

Asdrin had made a chamomile and pine tea to calm the nerves in camp. Kas then told them that the journey through the North Wood had its own perils. Apart from some unsavoury beasts, poisonous plants, carnivorous trees and so on, there was talk of a Soul Reaper having taken up residence in this dark place. None of the group asked for an explanation of the Reaper's skillset but suffice to say that they didn't want to run into this abhorrence. Having finished their refreshments, they packed up their belongings and hit the trail, going deeper into the unfamiliar and foreboding territory.

They eventually came to a fork in the path, using a coin toss to make the choice of which route to take. "So much for scientific reasoning!" Alex muttered.

"Explain 'science'?" Kas replied.

With an eager exuberance, Alex said, "Well, we look for the truth in everything by systematic reasoning and applied theory…" He was cut off by Kas.

"Coin tossing has got me out of many a perilous situation." He laughed at his own statement whilst apologizing to Alex for cutting her off.

Asdrin had stopped up ahead. Kas went to speak, his brother motioned for him to be quiet; they all went on alert. Kas and the others caught up with Asdrin, he spoke in a soft whisper. "We are being followed on all sides, but I don't know by how many."

"See what happens when you toss coins?" There was a large chunk of sarcasm in Alex's words.

"What is your business in the black woods, warriors?" Only one voice spoke but there was enough menace in it to chill their blood. Faldor growled deep in his throat. Kas spoke first. "Can you not speak face to face or are you a coward?" He spat the last word out as a direct challenge.

"Who are the outlanders that you bring to my land?" Again, there was a threat in what the faceless speaker was saying. Kas stepped forward.

"If you wish to harm them then there will be blood spilled at this very spot, I warn you now. Show yourself or prepare to meet your ancestors." Kas had gone very still, waiting to leap to action. Jade took Alex's hand.

"Whatever comes, don't leave my side." She nodded. There was a noise behind them.

"Veldan, always looking for a fight?" The voice now had a face; there was a young man standing in the middle of the path. He was dressed in a simple hessian-style cloth with leather ankle boots and a small leather pouch. His hair was jet black and under it he had a slim face with high cheek bones, but it was his eyes that caught their attention, black with no pupils. Kas swung round, putting his friends behind him whilst levelling his sword at the intruder's chest.

"As I said, lay…" His hand was on fire, or at least that was what it felt like. He looked down at his sword; it was glowing bright orange.

"I've had enough of your threats and your wolf, Veldan!" Kas took Asdrin's arm, holding him back from the creature.

"What is your name, imp?" The intruder stepped forward. As he did, Kas's sword leaped from the ground into his hand. Everything went still.

"You may know me as the Soul Reaper." Everyone held their breath, including Kas. "But you can call me Finn." He handed Kas the sword and looked him in the eye. "I fight the same enemy as you and your friends." They were all stunned.

Chapter Sixteen

Appearing to comply with director Grearson's request, Tom had taken a few days away from the CERN facility and was actual enjoying being free of his responsibilities. Even so, he was still plotting a way to get back at the good professor. He toured around the local area taking some time to go hiking and sampling the local cuisine and hospitality, which to him was adequate. On the fourth night, however, the nightmares came back with renewed vigour. It was as if Dante had been let loose on his subconscious. "You are running out of time," the voice boomed inside his mind, "Open the gateway and you shall have all that I have promised." He had shown Tom visions of the things that Tom desired; power, wealth, fame and respect, the latter most of all.

Although an acclaimed scientist, he had always felt that he could have been so much more than a teaching professor. "Fucking Grearson, what's that old son of a bitch done apart from sit behind his desk and act like God? It's me who should be there calling the shots." Tom talked out loud; luckily, he was driving at the time.

He was heading back to the facility hoping the director would see that he had cleaned up and was back with the program, so to speak. His dark mentor had a plan for the good professor Grearson. After clearing security, Tom headed straight to Grearson's office. On entering the building, he went to the bank of elevators and pressed the call button on both sides. There was a familiar ping and the doors opened. Stepping inside, he pressed the button for level four and the doors closed. That hum associated with all elevator journeys played on his way to the top floor. Ping: the noise snapped him from his thoughts as the doors slid open. He was confronted with the director himself. "Tom, back early?" Grearson didn't hesitate as he stepped inside the elevator Tom was half out of when he noticed his boss.

"Director Grearson, I was just on my way to see you." There was nervousness in Tom's voice. He had practiced his conversation on the drive up but was now totally off script and on the back foot.

"Nice to see you've shaved and have dressed in the proper manner for a man in your position. I trust the time given to you has had the desired effect?"

"Yes, er, yes, things are, er, a lot better. I've had enough rest and need to get on with my work." The director stopped the elevator, looking straight at Tom as he spoke clearly.

"I appreciate that you want to get back quickly, but a week is a week. Unless you've been working on a way to compress time, you've still got a few more days of rest to take." The way the statement was said tipped Tom over the edge.

"For fuck's sake, Paul, if I say I'm fit to fucking work, then I am!" Tom was shaking as he spoke. His boss hit the button to start the elevator moving. As they reached the bottom, he engaged Tom again.

"I've made my position clear on this subject, Tom, and I don't care for your tone or your language. If you don't take the rest of your time, I may have to refer you for a psychological evaluation, which at this moment looks like my only option." The doors opened and the director walked away without looking back. Tom stood in silence and stayed inside as the elevator made its return trip upwards.

Chapter Seventeen

Finn, as it turned out, was from a long line of spell-keepers, a wizard of sorts. He had been waiting on their arrival; tales of the black witch Marsan Crissdan had reached his order and Finn had volunteered to be their guardian. He had used the Soul Reaper guise to keep the North Wood free of unwanted visitors and anyone who would jeopardise their quest. As they talked, Alex told him what had happened so far, especially her latest experience with the darkness. Finn sat patiently till Alex had finished then he began speaking again. "The journey you are on has been attempted by many; all have failed." Alex had a knot in the pit of her stomach as Finn continued. "They didn't succeed but not for their lack of courage. They failed because they did not have the correct bloodline. You, Alex McDonald, have the proper lineage, that's part of it, and what you carry is another." Finn pointed to Alex's amulet. "This evil held within your pendant governs not only your destiny but the lives of all of us. Because of your lineage, you alone can bear the heavy burden that is attached to it. Be it a talisman, or a parchment, or a ring, pure evil has many forms, but its goal is simple; to find its maker, the Dark One."

They all sat in silence waiting for the next piece of the puzzle. The spell-keeper spoke but this time there was a warning in his tone. "These episodes you have been experiencing are its way of trying to break free and although your bloodline is strong, you will be tested, and it is looking for a weakness right now as we speak. Your courage and that of your friends will be tested also. I tell you this not to put fear in your heart but to strengthen your purpose and to see this out till its conclusion." The group of friends sat with mixed emotions wondering what to make of the stranger's words.

Alex was first to speak.

"How do we know that what you have just told us is true?" She looked Finn in the eye.

"Unfortunately, you don't..." He looked at their faces. "It is your choice to accept me as guardian; it is your decision and yours alone. If you choose not to have me, then I wish you well on the road ahead." Finn moved away leaving the others to speak. Kas replied first.

"I've been trained as a healer and Finn feels right to me. And Faldor hasn't eaten him yet so he must be on our side." The friends laugh. Asdrin spoke next.

"I don't have my brother's insight but if he says so then I agree."

Alex was looking at Jade waiting for an answer. When she spoke, there was truth in her words.

"I think that any journey that is as perilous as this one, means we need to work together."

They reached the half-way point in good time and would spend one more night in the woods. The group had gotten into their making-camp routine. While Asdrin was gathering herbs and berries, Kas showed Jade how to trap while she also hunted with her bow. Alex was making a fire and Finn, trying to find his place within the group, used a couple of large clear pebbles as lighting, placing the glowing rocks in holes left in the tree trunk. Alex asked Finn about his powers; he told her that his magic was only to be used sparingly on practical things like the lights, as the more illumination you had in the woods at night, the better it was for all. He also told Alex that not squandering his power kept him in balance with his environment and allowed him to use powerful spells when the situation dictated. Finn's explanation seemed logical.

Over the evening, they got to know Finn better as he told

them tales of the adventures that had brought him onto their path. Alex spoke of the Scottish Highlands and the modern world that both herself and Jade lived in. Kas and Asdrin were fascinated by some of the stories that Alex told them. Kas then explained that they would have to pass through the heart of North Wood tomorrow; it was the oldest part of the woodland. There were tales of its dark past that would be told as Kas and Asdrin were growing up; stories of sorcery, magic and strange creatures that used to walk its darkest paths.

After a restful night and a good breakfast, they broke camp. Gathering their belongings together, the group tried to leave the glade in as good a state as they had found it. There were some routines that were upheld no matter what realm you travelled to and this one was no different. As the friends walked, they would gather food, berries and the like. Kas would name tree types and their uses or dangers, while Finn asked everyone a lot of questions, but in a nice and friendly way. Jade had braided her hair with a piece of leather through it, which made her look even more like a local. Alex was thinking; she'd been running recent events over in her head and questioned some of the choices she'd made. Jade had noticed Alex had gone quiet and came over to talk. "Penny for your thoughts?" Alex half smiled at her.

"No. Nothing really, just going over stuff, thinking about my parents and grandparents. I'm sorry for dragging you into this mess." Jade cut her off mid-sentence.

"You didn't drag me into anything, I volunteered." Her smile beamed and she hoped it would snap her out of this gloom.

"The way I see it, you railroaded me into this and then took advantage of me sexually. I feel used." She grabbed Alex, pinning her shoulders to the ground.

"If these guys weren't here, I'd give you some more of

what you got back at your cottage."

"I'm trying to save the world and all you can think about is having your wicked way with me. You modern women, it's all sex, sex, sex." The pair laughed and giggled, enjoying a brief lull in the journey they had chosen.

Getting up, they found the others and continued going deeper into the mysterious North Wood. Their presence hadn't gone unnoticed.

At the heart of wood, the trees were many centuries old. They had seen countless wars, kings had come and gone, and they had survived them all. A long time ago, the trees had guardians who both protected and kept them in check. These keepers were now long dead, leaving the wood to its own devices. Being of nature, the wood's ancient heart was neither good nor evil; it just existed and would react to any perceived threat in a manner it deemed fit. The fact that Alex's amulet had entered the wood was now having an influence on how they were looked upon, which at this point wasn't in their favour. Like any good hunter, it let the prey or threat come within striking distance before unleashing its full power. The trap was set, waiting to snap shut at the right time. The North Wood had been born at the beginning of this realm; it knew how to be patient, so now it waited.

Little sunlight penetrated through to the canopy above. It was about time for the travelers to make camp again and they had gathered most of the food needed to feed them for their overnight stay. Even Faldor joined in bringing the odd rabbit and dropping it at Jade's feet. Needing only to collect some wood, they would make a fire consisting of a central six-to-eight-foot log then smaller tinder around it, which once aflame would ignite the larger piece and keep them warm throughout the night.

Alex was explaining or trying to explain mountaineering

to all but Jade. The others sat listening about all the mountains she'd climbed, with Jade agreeing when Alex mentioned a mountain that she herself had summated. The others sat perplexed; to them, scaling a peak was only done if it was an emergency or for finding a new route to a specific place. The fact that the outlanders did it for fun baffled and at the same time impressed them.

There was a comforting glow from the fire as Finn took his turn to watch over the others. He had a lot on his mind and enjoyed the quiet that being on guard duty offered. He knew that the journey ahead would be full of danger, which all depended on the choices of some of those who he watched over this very night. Finn, among his other talents, was blessed with foresight; he could see versions of events yet to come but nothing, as in life, was certain. As he sat watching the others sleep, there was a gnawing feeling of dread about the next morning's events.

There was a low-lying mist in the North Wood. Asdrin had fallen asleep on his guard duty but snapped out of it quickly when the shouting started. The problem for him was he could not see anyone through the mist and more to the point, he couldn't hear his brother. Lying in the dense mist, the group also awoke to the screaming; it was Jade then Alex and finally Finn who were all calling for assistance. Each of them had woken to find that they could not move, as if being held by some unseen entity. Even Faldor had been restrained.

Asdrin reached for his sword only to find his legs and weapon were held fast. Reaching down, his hands moved over what he thought was some sort of vegetation like ivy. Being only caught by his legs, he managed to slip out of his bonds, quickly moving towards the voices. He felt around blindly, trying to locate his companions. The first person he found was Alex, her body held down tightly by the vines. "Get me out of this crap!" There was urgency in her voice.

Asdrin pulled out his knife and started to cut, but that was a bad decision. Alex cried out. "Nooo!" she said as the tethers tightened. Asdrin frantically tried to find a way out of this predicament when he heard Alex's voice.

"Go to your pack, break a piece of the salt off, put it in water and come back here, quickly!" Asdrin rushed about in the mist, eventually finding his pack and the rock salt. He broke a piece off with the butt of his knife. He then found the water, dropped the salt in then stirred it vigorously to break up the mineral. Everything had suddenly gone quiet. Rushing back to Alex, her voice was but a whisper.

"Pour it on the vines, POUR IT ON THE VINES!" Asdrin complied with Alex's fearful demand. As soon as the water touched the vines, their pressure relinquished. Alex told Asdrin to free the others. One by one, they appeared through the mist, seemingly no worse for their ordeal. Kas immediately spoke.

"I have heard tales of these woods but had put most of them down to old wife's tales to keep children from wandering too far. It seems that they are true." They all looked at Alex.

"How did you know salt water would work to free its grip on you?" Asdrin asked him. Alex, still getting air into his lungs, spoke softly.

"We use it for killing weeds, plants that have no real function or invade your crops lowering its yield, do you understand?" They nodded. Kas looked at the group.

"If all the stories are true, about this place, then maybe it's time we push to get through to the other side." The others all agreed.

"Our journey is going to get tougher with more challenging situations to get through. I'm going to be honest, not all of us will see our homes again." Finn's words silenced the group, but they all knew that he had spoken the truth. They had all made a choice to face these dangers, but it did not take the edge off Finn's honest words. They made it to the other side of the North Wood without incident.

The next realm gate lay just ahead on a plateau ridge set into the mountainside. The group made their way up a boulder-filled path, all were thinking about the other side and a land that few had ventured to. Only the Veldan had contact with their other realm neighbours and even that was tenuous. The friends linked hands at the gateway, Kas removed her necklace and placed the charm in the relevant place then took Faldor by the fur on his neck. There was a pause then a familiar distortion. Alex held Jade's hand tightly then everything turned black once again.

Chapter Eighteen

"ALEX." Jade's voice forced Alex's eyes to snap open. After getting over the nausea of the shift and washing her mouth out, Alex kissed Jade then asked how the others were. Everyone bar Finn had suffered the nausea of the ride through. The travelers stood in a barren quarry basin, rain stinging their faces. Kas and Asdrin took the lead with Faldor running ahead as usual.

They made their way out of the quarry onto a flat plainland interspersed with small lochans (ponds) dotted here and there. Most of the area was rough grasslands, reminding Alex of the sheep grazing back home. The group made their way along the steep path leading down from the gateway, looking for some sort of cover to shelter and dry their clothes. They found an overhang and searched around for anything that could make a fire. Wood was scarce so most of what the group found was shrubs and heather, which they needed a lot of because it burned quickly. They made the fire against the rock face, which heated the stone and held the heat there for longer.

Resigned to spending a night under the rock face, they broke out their rations and boiled water for some heather tea. After eating their meager meal, they set out a plan of action. Kas and Asdrin oversaw negotiations with the Uddon, who were both tough seafarers and horsemen. Alex would have to meet with their leader, as all visitors had to, but this was an especially important moment in all their lives so it was imperative that she made her presence felt. The fire had done its job in keeping them warm throughout the night and as dawn broke, the rain subsided, and a bright red sun ushered the morning in. They hadn't travelled far from their campsite when the land opened into a flat basin with an open expanse of water stretching off as far as the eye could see. "Must be some kind of sea loch," Alex spoke, remembering similar landscapes back home.

"Lock?" Kas asked. Alex corrected him.

"No, it's pronounced 'loghhh', it's a Scots word for a lake." Alex continued, "A sea loch is a body of water that comes from the sea but cuts deep inland along the coastline. In our culture, there was a clan known as the Vikings who used these sea lochs as roads for trade. In war, they allowed them to move inland quickly to overrun their enemies." Both Kas and Asdrin were intrigued by the Vikings and thanked Alex again for sharing more tales of his world and its history.

Following the shoreline, they moved forward with a rough idea of where they had to go. Gorran had told them to follow the water inland and the Uddon would find them and escort them to their village.

The great bird soared high above the travelers, circled three times, then flew back inland, losing altitude as it did so. Their boat cut through the water like a stone skipping across a pond. There were twelve men rowing in time with each other, no words being spoken as they focused on the rhythm of their strokes. Their captain stood at the bow looking out over the water. There was movement out to the right; he raised his right arm clad in thick leather and, as he did so, the eagle swooped in, bracing its wings against the wind to land softly on his master's arm. There was no hood or leg tethers on the bird; he had never needed them. Tealuk had raised him from a young eaglet after his mother had been killed by lightning and had given the great bird his name, Storm, to remind himself of life and death. Their bond was unbreakable. He pointed the new direction to his men, and they immediately adjusted their course to where the bird had been circling. Someone or something had encroached on his land, a mistake on their part.

Faldor looked out across the loch. Kas warned the others, "Someone is coming." Keeping his eyes focused on the small boat, he told the others to let him do all the talking. Kas had been with his father on a previous meeting, he had a rough idea of how to handle things, or so he hoped. With a final stroke, the men stowed their oars and coasted to shore. "Kas, son of Gorran. What brings you to our shores?" Tealuk's voice had no threat in it. Looking deep into the other man's face, he recognised him from his last trip.

"Teelik?" he inquired.

"Close enough, it's Tealuk, we met when you were last here with your father." Kas nodded in agreement. He looked over his shoulder at the boat with the eagle perched on the carved bow post.

"Your eagle has grown as much as you have, Tealuk." The others introduced themselves as Tealuk gazed at the charm on Alex's neck.

"There are many who would ruin all we have to put that around their necks. You are indeed brave to carry such a weighty burden." Alex thanked him for his kind words.

Kas inquired about Tealuk's father, Rahan, and was told he was gravely ill and that his brother, Tealuk's uncle Braunn, had taken over as guardian of the realm. As he talked, the others could sense an unease in his words, but none spoke out, fearing they would bring shame to the young man.

Finn, who had been surprisingly quiet till now, asked if he could see Tealuk's father. Kas also offered his help in a healing capacity. Tealuk was overwhelmed but kept his dignity while accepting their gifts.

The journey inland took them through a fjord with sheer cliffs either side that must have been one to two thousand feet high, or so Alex guessed. The grey slabs of rock reminded her of the adventure on the rock face in Glencoe and that feeling of being pursued, which had only become worse the deeper into this adventure she'd gotten. Alex had kept this from Jade – from everyone for that matter – choosing to bear that burden on her own. Now as they moved closer to the Uddon's Keep, Alex's intuition was telling her that something was wrong. Something gnawed deep within her. She sat debating whether to tell the others and decided that when they reached shore, the best thing for all of them would be complete clarity. Jade interrupted her thinking. "Where were you off to? You seemed a million miles away just now." Alex's gaze dropped into the bottom of the boat before she spoke.

"Just got something on my mind. I'll talk to you guys when we get back on terra firma." Jade didn't push Alex for an answer as she could see Alex was in an emotional turmoil. All Jade did was reach out and take hold of her hand and give it a soft squeeze. As she did this, they both looked ahead towards Uddon's Keep which, as they got closer, dominated the horizon.

Kas, Asdrin and Finn were glad to disembark from the boat, not being natural sailors. They all looked at the vast structure of the Keep as the boat came to a stop. The shoreline was packed with at least a dozen vessels of various sizes and to their right was a stockade full of horses. On the other side various animals kept in small pens lined the main access road, which wound its way up to a set of massive wooden outer gates. On either side of the gates were small fields with different grain crops, of which some were about ready to harvest. The rest still had time for the seed to brown and swell.

The most striking feature sat back from the Keep a few miles inland; a volcano, rising to a dizzy height. Its summit was partially hidden in the clouds and covered in snow, and there was a small trace of smoke that reached up to the sky from the right-hand side. Their eyes were drawn back down to Tealuk, who welcomed them all to his lands. "This is Sjernvogst, this is my home."

He told them that Sjernvogst translated as 'Keeper of the Fire' or fire mountain. The volcano kept them warm in the winter and they used the heat off it to grow some crops in heated caves that kept them in fresh vegetables throughout the year. "I'd love to see that, Tealuk," Alex inquired.

"Yes, Alex, but first you must all pay your respects to my uncle. After that, Kas and Finn can tend to my father then I'll show you the caves. Even you, Faldor," Tealuk replied. He reached down to touch the dog but let him sniff his hand first before ruffling the hair on its head. With a quick whistle, Storm flew up onto his master's arm watched closely by Faldor.

As they approached the gate, they could see it was made of great slabs of wood and steel which opened with an ominous low creak. Once inside, the doors were pulled back into place by two teams of oxen. Whoever designed the gate had done so with a good deal of thought; they opened outwardly and locked tight when closed, which meant in a siege there was no chance of breaching the gates with a battering ram. Any attacker would have to smash their way in, which would leave ample time for the Keep's defenders to pick their enemies apart from the ramparts.

The Keep's main building seemed to grow out of the grey granite walls of the fjord. Massive block pillars led to an arched doorway that was open at this moment. The roof consisted of large main beams with smaller ones that supported roof boards, on top of which the outer wood shingles were nailed. Dropping down from the main beams were circular candelabra that could be winched into place when the candles were lit. Here and there, tapered flags bearing the Uddon emblem, a long boat, hung on poles occasionally moving whenever a breeze was passing. Deeper still into the bowels of the Keep, the main water supply came from an internal river that came down from high in the cliff walls and ended in a waterfall in the main building. Internal shafts and polished metal mirrors supplied light to the inner halls and chambers; this truly was an amazing construction.

Tealuk left Storm outside his uncle's day room and Kas followed suit with Faldor. As he entered, his uncle beckoned him. "Tealuk, where have you been and who are your new friends?" There was an edge of sarcasm, anger, and threat in his uncle's voice; everybody noticed it.

Tealuk's elder was a mountain of a man. His physique was on the low side of large, probably due to his over-indulgent eating after taking over from Tealuk's father as decision-maker for the Uddon. When Tealuk spoke, he had an authority of a confident young heir.

"Uncle," he began. Tealuk knew not to use his name, Braunn. "These realm folks are our guests, they represent the Veldan, the McDonalds and…" Tealuk turned to Finn, gesturing for him to tell him his home realm. Finn paused for a moment then said he was from Kroen.

"Sorcerer," bellowed Tealuk's uncle. Finn stepped forward.

"I am no sorcerer," he replied in a steady voice, "but I do have a talent with magic."

Tealuk looked at his uncle. The room had gone deathly quiet. Before he spoke, Braunn finished the piece of meat he held then wiped both hands with a small cloth from the table.

"I have yet to meet a man of magic who has brought value to me and my kin." The older man spat the words out along with some of the meat he'd just consumed. Again, Finn spoke in a soft tone, deliberately trying not to provoke a confrontation with Tealuk's uncle.

"Hopefully someday I can change your view on magic

and its uses." Finn bowed and stepped backwards to join the rest of the group.

Braunn stood up and crossed the room. As he did so, he looked everyone in the eye then settled on Alex's. His gaze dropped to the young woman's neck and the gold talisman she wore. Braunn spoke again, his eyes re-engaged with Alex's.

"Our realms have paid the price countless times over the centuries for the misuse of magic and objects of dark power. Knowing that I speak not only for my brother on this matter, but we also want none of your magic practiced within these walls." Braunn finished his sentence, his eyes once again fell on Finn. This left an uneasy feeling in the pit of the young wizard's stomach.

Chapter Nineteen

"Professor Johansen, Professor Johansen!" Director Grearson's secretary Anne had called his name twice, but Tom was lost in his own thoughts. Tom apologized to her. "Director Grearson will see you now." Tom thanked Anne then gave a polite knock on the door and entered. Paul Grearson was looking out at the beautiful view from his window. He took a deep breath then let it out and turned his chair around.

"Tom, please take a seat. How are you feeling?" Tom picked up the quite different tone in his superior's voice and as he spoke, he noticed an uncertainty in his own.

"Er, um, fine!" Tom's brain was running fast; straight away, he was on the back foot.

Grearson's plan was to take control of this meeting; their previous encounters had been messy and that had to stop, now.

"Professor Johansen, I've been having a little think about your current situation, and I feel that it is putting far too much pressure on you…"

'No, no, no, no…' Tom thought.

"I'm suspending you from your teaching position as of today…" Grearson thought it best to be very direct; the time for diplomacy had come and gone.

Tom's world came crashing around him. Trying to put a logical slant on things and regain his composure, he asked the director, "And what about my own personal experiment, are you going to cancel that?" The director's next words brought salvation to Tom's crumbling world.

"Professor Johansen. Tom. I've known you for a few years now, as I have most of the teaching staff. You are an excellent scientist and theorist, but I think the pressures of teaching have taken their toll on you. We don't want to lose your brilliance,"

Grearson lied, "I feel it would be unfair of me to cut you from the program altogether. You can continue to work on your experiments and maybe in the future we can get you teaching again on, say, a part-time basis, what do you think?"

At that moment, Tom thought, 'You don't want to know what I'm thinking RIGHT NOW…' He held his temper back.

"Director Grearson, I can't thank you enough for recognizing that I was… struggling…" Now it was Tom's turn to lie. "And also, for allowing me to continue my very important experiments. If I was in your position, I don't know that I could have been so sympathetic, but I suppose that is why you are running the show and not me."

Paul listened to Tom. He knew that the scientist was trying to save his own skin, but what Tom didn't know was that the director had already made up a shortlist of suitable candidates to replace him. Paul had initially recommended Tom to the board and felt a responsibility to rectify that mistake.

The two men shook hands and the director escorted Tom to the door. Grearson even managed to put a friendly hand on the professor's shoulder as they walked, although the longer he left it there, the more it made his flesh crawl. So much so that when he said farewell to Tom and went back into his office, he washed his hands thoroughly in scalding water.

'Not long now!' Tom mused as he rode down in the elevator, 'Soon the likes of Grearson will be nothing but fertilizer for the new order of things.'

"Not long now…" The last part of his sentence echoed off the walls of the elevator, but he didn't care – his only focus now was to do his dark mentor's bidding. "Soon the world will know, soon the world will know."

Bing: the elevator doors opened, and Professor Johansen greeted the new occupant with a hearty "Good morning!" before walking in the direction of his office.

Chapter Twenty

Kas and Finn looked down at the old man lying in the bed. Tealuk's father King Rahan was gravely ill, his skin grey and drawn. The two men moved closer and opened his eyelids; the eyes were showing white, and he was barely breathing, just short breaths but very shallow. Finn checked his visible flesh for any trauma, finding a small festering scratch on the back of Rahan's left hand. He drew Kas' attention to it. Their eyes locked for a moment then they turned to Tealuk. "Your father is near death." Finn's words were to the point and Tealuk respected him for it. "He is not long for this world but there is worse news. We think he has been poisoned."

The young heir sat down on his father's bed. When he spoke, he only said one word; "How?" Turning to Kas and Finn for answers, the men looked at each other hoping the other would take the lead. Finally, it was Finn who spoke.

"There is a flower common in the realms for its medicinal value but like most plants of this type, there is a dark side to their natural healing properties. If distilled to the correct potency, they can be deadly." Both men showed Tealuk the scratch on his father's hand. The young man was confused.

"Who would do this and why?" They all looked at each other but no one spoke. Tealuk whispered one name, "Braunn!" Finn spoke again, trying to reassure the young prince.

"There is one plant that can reverse these symptoms. We call it Dove's Foot because the flower resembles the birds' appendage."

Tealuk told them there was one place they could find this; on the north face of the volcano where the heat in the rocks made it bloom all year.

Later, Alex and Kas volunteered to fetch the plant and Tealuk gave them one of his most trusted men, Qi, to guide them where they needed to go.

As Tealuk promised, he showed them the heated caves where they grew crops throughout the year thanks to the volcanic vents and an ingenious system of mirrors that brought light from outside deep into the caves. Alex thought this was magnificent.

"There is a country back home called Iceland. They have lots of volcanoes and use the vents to heat their homes and water, but they have nothing like this."

Tealuk showed them the rest of the Keep and then outside where they kept some oxen-type cattle, chickens, and the horses. There was a group of young men trying to break a young colt, the scene one of total chaos. One man was on the animal's head, another clinging to its tail, then a third was trying to hobble or tie its front legs together. The young colt was screaming for its life, thrashing, and kicking anything or anyone within reach. Tealuk laughed and shouted abuse at his kinsmen, mocking their skill. Jade, on the other hand, was furious; she called out to the warriors. "Call yourself horsemen? You're just savages." There was nothing but rage and utter contempt in her words.

Alex gently took her arm, but Jade shrugged her off. She then did something none of them expected. Jumping over the corral fence and walked up to Tealuk's men. "Stop this butchery and give me the horse!" They all looked at Tealuk and he gave them a nod.

Jade took the line attached to the rope halter, speaking softly to the young colt who was charging this way and that trying to find a way out. Jade matched his movements, still talking quietly to the angry horse. The colt went to the end of the line, which was about twenty feet long, and started to drag Jade. The warriors found this most amusing and shouted encouragement to her but in a sarcastic tone. She ignored them and continued to work on the colt. Running out of room, the horse turned and ran straight at Jade, causing Alex to call out to her. Jade ignored her.

The colt towered over her, rearing up on his back legs before striking out at her head. Jade moved out of the way of each strike, finally pulling the line to the side to take the horse's balance, which made him stumble and stop dead in his tracks. The warriors had gone silent. Alex and the others watched as she quietly walked up to the colt and lay her hand on his forehead. The young horse let out a huge sigh then lowered his head. Jade continued to speak softly to her charge as she worked her hands down both of his sides. There was a growing crowd watching as she worked with the horse.

Next, Jade walked down his side towards his hind quarters and as she reached them, his head came around and in behind her, followed by the rest of his body. Jade was leading and he followed. Every now and then, she would turn around sharply, causing the young horse to stop in his tracks. Each time he did this, she would come into him and rub his forehead and tell him he was a "good lad". Next, she put him on a circle then changed directions a few times before going back in behind at the end of each task. Alex, Asdrin, Tealuk and everyone else watching couldn't believe what they were seeing; it was mesmerizing and beautiful to watch how they interacted with each other.

What Jade did next no one there that day would ever forget. She slipped the rope halter off then coiled the rope up, keeping it in her hand. Wherever she walked, the colt would follow. They circled, went straight, backed up, and did it all again in trot. Jade slipped the halter back on then led the horse to the corral fence and proceeded to climb up onto the top rail. Once there, she guided the colt into position then sat down gently on his back. She held onto his mane and asked him to walk forward, which he did, then again. Jade walked him around the corral then did it in trot.

Taking the horse to the centre of the corral, Jade dismounted. Again, she slipped the halter off then walked in the direction of Alex and the others, the colt tagging along till they got to the fence line. Jade stopped, turned around, and took his head in her hands, kissing him on the forehead to thank him for letting her be the first. With that, she ducked under the rail. Tealuk bowed his head. "I and my kinsmen have been humbled by your true horsemanship. Please forgive us all for our brutality."

"I can forgive but only the horse and you can do that with purpose," Jade responded, "I can teach you what I know." Tealuk and his men nodded in agreement.

Alex was dumbfounded. "Where did you learn to do that?" Jade laughed then playfully punched Alex on the arm.

"Me? I'm full of surprises." Then it was Asdrin's turn to compliment her.

"Jade, you have some skill with a horse. Most people who saw what you did would say it was witchcraft!" Jade laughed again and thanked him. She then told them about her grandfather who was an old horseman, telling her all the old stories of when he'd work with various horses over the years and that had sparked her interest.

"Alex, don't you remember my pony, Poppy?"

"Vaguely," she replied, "But that was when you were a kid!"

"Well, I always kept my interest over the years and one time I got to train with an old cowboy from the States. He showed me this style of training where we work with the horse, not against it. If I hadn't been an architect, I would probably have worked with horses, that and a bit of mountaineering." Tealuk asked Jade if there was time.

"Maybe tomorrow," she suggested. He asked if she could come down again and instruct his men in her style. "Sure, I can."

The horses and other beasts were becoming restless. Tealuk was walking them back to show where their sleeping quarters would be when the ground began to shake. As quick as it had started, it stopped. Alex looked at Tealuk.

"Does that happen a lot?"

"It's the mountain god, he's hungry." Then he laughed. The others joined in except for Alex.

"What's up?" Jade asked.

"Sometimes prior to an eruption you get a lot of mini tremors like that one. They are like an early warning system for the main event."

Tealuk asked, "Eruption?"

"When the mountain blows up," Alex explained. She used her hands to add to the previous description.

Tealuk told them he had seen this once before but on a different volcano. He said that it looked like his realm was coming to an end and the others nodded in agreement. Alex then asked him if there had been many tremors before this one. Tealuk told her there had been some but more over the last few weeks. Alex's gut instinct went into overdrive, but she kept it from the others, choosing to simply nod as she was told this. Jade didn't buy it but would talk to her later.

The young warrior showed his guests to their room and bid them good day. The room was massive with their own sunken bath that had a constant flow of hot water coming in at one end and leaving by the overflow at the other. It had its own latrine, wash bowl and polished metal mirrors. The bed and chairs were made of wood with decorative cloth and cushions on both. Jade put her arms around Alex's neck. "Are you going to tell me when the volcano is going to blow?" Alex was quiet for a while but when she spoke, it put Jade in the picture.

"I think the magma is rising now. It can do this and cause tremors. There is no eruption, but I've got a feeling that this one is different and could be deadly. The thing I've got in my head is I could warn Tealuk and his people, but I'll probably sound like a madman or worse, a sorcerer."

Jade could feel the tension in Alex's body; this was serious. She let her talk some more before asking, "How long do we, they, have?" Her reply was vague.

"How long's a piece of string? It could be weeks, days or worst-case scenario, hours."

Alex, Kas, and Qi waited at the gates of the keep. Tealuk, Jade and Asdrin, went to bid them farewell. "Qi will guide you on the quickest path, may your journey be a swift one my friends. Tealuk bowed and walked back inside the gates.

Alex hugged Jade, "We won't be long, Asdrin is here if you need anything." Asdrin nodded in the background.

"Please hurry, I don't trust this Braunn, he gives me the creeps." Jade hugged Alex a last time then, like Tealuk, vanished inside the great oak gates.

In her room, Jade was trying to rest when there was a knock on his door. "Come in," she said, sitting up. The door swung open to reveal a young man, a messenger.

"My lord would like to talk to you in his chambers." Jade thanked the young man and asked him to wait outside the door.

Jade was wondering what Braunn wanted to talk about as she followed the messenger through the corridors of the Keep;

why not wait till Alex was back? The boy knocked softly on his master's door. Braunn shouted "enter" before the young messenger opened the door and ushered Jade in.

"Dear friend, come in, take a seat, wine?" Jade was courteous and accepted the drink. "Alex is wise to have such a strong woman in her council." Asdrin thanked Braunn for the compliment, also being wary of what tack the conversation was taking. Braunn continued.

"It is never easy being in the shadows. Take me for instance, my older sibling always gets the biggest share of a father's affection." The older man paused to see if Jade agreed with him; she didn't say anything.

"I've been fortunate enough to assist my brother in his hour of need and maybe someday you will do the same for Alex." Keeping her calm, Jade replied to Braunn.

"Alex is indeed strong and someone to whom I will pledge my life for." Jade would not be drawn in to play the game of the elder statesman.

Braunn applauded Jade's loyalty. "Alex was lucky to have such an obedient friend."

"I am my own woman." Jade glared at Braunn for his insult. The older man noticed this and changed the subject.

"These trinkets your friend wants, we have them, all of them." Jade was surprised, it had been long thought that the charms were still held by individual realm kings.

"You have them here?" Braunn laughed.

"You sound surprised, my young friend. I have been entrusted by the other realms to hold these powerful talismans till a time comes when they can be dealt with." Something in what Braunn said didn't add up to Jade but without Alex's counsel, she could not take any action. Plus, they were in a strange land far from home and were vastly outnumbered. She had to think quickly. There was a lengthy pause between them, which Jade finally broke.

"You must be a trusted ambassador to have been given such a weighty task." Jade's voice held steady even though she felt an increasing pressure from her host. Braunn pressed some more.

"Alex, she has a similar amulet to the ones I have, yes?" Jade could see where this conversation was going, and she tried to halt it.

"These evil things need to be destroyed; it's why you were given the rest by the other kings. We have only one chance at this, surely you can see that?" The steward rose from his seat and poured Jade another drink. He put his hand on her shoulder, his hands wandered towards her breasts.

"All I... we, want is that pendant. You can destroy the others. In helping me to get it, I can give you anything you've ever wanted or needed." Jade felt like she was standing on very thin ice; one false move and she would be in trouble. Jade desperately needed to talk to Alex, but she would have to let this play out for now.

"What you're asking me to do has big consequences for me and I'm sure you can appreciate I would need time to think about it," she lied, buying time. Braunn nodded. Jade shrugged off the older man's advances, then he spoke.

"I'll give you a day to think things over."

Jade sat in the room whittling a small piece of wood. There was a knock on their door, Asdrin entered, closing the door behind him. Jade threw the carving on the fire. "Is there anything wrong Jade?" He asked.

She told him of her meeting with Braunn and the deal that was offered. Asdrin was shocked at this development. He told her that he would try to speak to Tealuk at the evening meal but until then they should act as naturally as possible.

"Braunn is working for the Darkness, we have to find out if Tealuk's men are loyal to him and his father or if they have secretly changed allegiance and joined the other side." Jade asked him,

"Can we not just give them the amulet?" Asdrin's words were cold and blunt.

"If I give up the amulet then we and all that is good in the realms and our world will be lost."

High on the volcano, Alex, Kas, and their new friend Qi had reached their destination. They gathered the flowers then wrapped them in a flannel and put it in a leather pouch. After they were done, the men started back down the slope. Something was wrong. Faldor had stopped in his tracks and was looking Kas straight in the eye. He was about to call the dog back when there was a massive tremor, causing all of them to fall to the ground. Above them to their right, a fissure opened and tracked downwards parallel to where they lay. Sulphur gas filled the air as the three men got to their feet and set off again.

Just as they had gotten back on the trail, there was another huge tremor along with more gas. Sizeable rocks came hurtling down the mountain side as Qi shouted at his two companions, "Look out!" He flung his body against them, knocking both out of the path of the massive boulder that then hit Qi square in the chest and pushed him over the side of the mountain. Qi was dead before falling.

Alex and Kas looked over where their companion had fallen. He was five hundred or so feet down, lying like a child's doll that had fallen to the ground. Kas said a short prayer that sped the warrior's spirit across to the other side. He looked at Alex then spoke. "He was a brave man."

"The bravest," Alex replied, "We must get off this cursed

mountain and quickly." Kas nodded in agreement. They picked up their pace and headed down as if chased by the Darkness himself.

"Your uncle wants my amulet in exchange for the others." As Asdrin spoke, Tealuk's blood ran cold. He knew his uncle wanted his father's throne but now this. He looked at the faces of the others.

"This needs to stop. I will warn my most trusted men and keep them ready for the time that we make our move. I feel that I have let my father and the people down for long enough, we must put an end to this!" The handle on the door moved then it creaked open.

"Spies," Tealuk whispered as he drew his sword. Alex entered the room followed by Kas; they were greeted by cold steel. Alex placed her hand on the flat of Tealuk's sword, laughing at the same time.

"I'd hate to be your enemy, young man!"

"Where's Qi?" Tealuk greeted them as he looked over their shoulders for the third member of the party.

"Qi is gone, killed on the mountain saving our lives." Kas told Tealuk that he'd given Qi's spirit a proper blessing as it had moved to the other side.

"Thank you. Qi will grow stronger in the halls of our ancestors and will forever be remembered here for his strength and sacrifice."

Finn left to work on the cure for the poison. Tealuk himself went to find out which warriors were loyal to King Rahan. Jade told Alex and Kas what had been happening in their absence. Kas was proud of Asdrin.

"A lesser warrior would have challenged Braunn. You are truly worthy of the throne of Veldan!" Asdrin was stunned by his brother's comment.

"Surely, brother, you will be the next king of the Veldan?" There was a broad smile across Kas' face.

"I am and always will be a warrior but like all good fighters, a king needs to know how to heal as well as destroy. You will make a better king than I ever could. Father sees this too." The brothers embraced each other then went to see if Finn had completed his task.

In his room, Finn had just finished mixing the ingredients. He then strained them through a piece of linen, which left him with a kind of herbal tea. It was this brew that they hoped would cure the king. Pouring the precious liquid into two vials, he then screwed the corks in tight and put one in his leather pouch. The other he hid on the candelabra hanging from the ceiling, just in case. Leaving the room, he met Kas, Asdrin, then Tealuk, who asked if he'd managed to make the cure. "I have, Tealuk, and I suggest we give it to your father as quickly as possible." Tealuk and the others agreed.

"Where's Alex and Jade?" Asdrin asked.

"They must still be in their room," said Kas. Asdrin offered to go fetch them then meet the others in the king's chamber; they all agreed.

Asdrin left to fetch Alex, Tealuk took the rest of the group into his father's chambers. He asked the king's maid to leave the room then closed the door. His father looked worse than he did before. Tealuk asked Finn to administer the potion. Lifting his father's head and supporting him, he then motioned to Finn to come forwards. Just as he did so, the door burst open; it was Braunn with half a dozen guards.

"Seize them," he barked. Tealuk became enraged.

"Uncle, what is the meaning of this?" Braunn smiled.

"Your so-called friends were about to poison the king. If it weren't for this maid's quick thinking, he would have been lost. Your choice of acquaintance is poor and the fact that this one," he pointed to Finn, "is a sorcerer should have been your first warning. Take them away." As the guards seized Finn and Kas, they shouted their protests. This drew the attention of Asdrin, Jade and Alex, who by this time had made it to the room.

"What is this?" Alex asked.

"Uncle thinks Finn and Kas were trying to poison my father," Tealuk replied.

"That's nonsense, they were trying to cure him!" Alex shouted.

"With this?" Braunn held up the vial then smashed it on the ground. "You are lucky I don't throw all of you in the dungeons as it is. Your friends will spend time there before they are executed!" Braunn's final words sent a chill through all of them.

Tealuk tried to defend them, but his uncle had made his mind up. The rest of the group were confined to their rooms till the steward had decided what to do with them. Even Faldor was thrown in the Keep's kennels in his own private cell.

Asdrin, Jade and Alex were in their rooms pondering what to do about the present predicament, with Finn and Kas having been taken into the bowels of the Keep. They were thrown into individual cells that were damp and hot. If you were left there for any length of time, you would die of heat exhaustion. Kas shouted to Finn. "Save your strength, my friend Alex will find a way to get us out."

"I know." Finn thought back to his earlier vision and could now see that the events that were unfolding were part of what was happening now. He would keep this from the others till the time was right.

Later that evening, Braunn sent for Tealuk. His uncle sat

with a flagon of ale and beckoned his nephew to join him. "I think under the circumstances that being cooperative with me would be in you and your friends' interests." This wasn't a veiled threat. "If you get that amulet for me, in return I can promise that you will not join your friends in the dungeons on a charge of treason!"

Tealuk was enraged. "You know who poisoned my father, your king and brother. If you want that ring, you can do your own dirty work. I don't care what you do with me. Some day at some time, the people you serve will find out about your treachery and you will be held accountable for your actions." Tealuk had held onto these words for so long that as he spoke to them, he felt his body being purged of all the negativity his uncle's actions had caused.

Braunn shook his head then looked at the guard; he never spoke a word. His men took Tealuk by the arms and led him away to the cells. As he sat drinking his ale, Braunn thought about the amulet, its power, and how he could serve his master once he had taken it from the outlanders.

When they were out of sight, the guards let go of Tealuk. "We are loyal to your father, sire, along with many of the guards. Too long has the steward sat on your father's throne tainting it with his evil will." The young heir sent his men to guard the others as he went to speak to Finn and Kas.

On his way to the dungeons, he stopped to arm himself just in case the situation arose. On entering the dungeon, he met more guards who also pledged themselves to him – 'news travels fast,' he thought. Soon his uncle would know so his action must be swift. He got to the cells where they were keeping his friends and released them immediately. Upon being freed, Finn let Tealuk know that there was one vial of the potion left that could cure his father. Tealuk set off for Finn's quarters with haste and the renewed hope that he would bring the king back from the edge of the afterlife. Kas and Finn were tasked with helping the guards to create a diversion so that Tealuk could get to his father and administer the cure.

Braunn fueled with ale set out for Alex's room. He would take the charm by fair means or foul; it would be his by the end of this day.

Asdrin and Kas along with two of Tealuk's men set a series of small fires inside of the Keep's main reception halls and living quarters; this pulled enough attention as well as a few guards to allow Tealuk time to enter his father's room.

In the king's chamber, Tealuk took the cork from the vial then tipping his head forward poured the contents into his father's mouth. He coughed slightly as Tealuk lay his head back on the pillow. "Father, if you can hear me, we need your guidance now."

There was a commotion in the corridor, a fight. Alex reached for her sword just as the door exploded inward, catching Jade in the process, sending her into the wall and out cold. "Bastard," Alex shouted on seeing Braunn in the doorway.

"I've come for that charm, scum, and when I'm finished with you, she," he pointed to Jade, "will be next to feel my sword inside her!"

Braunn lunged at Alex, who sidestepped the clumsy attack, sending the Braunn flying into the table at the far side of the room. Alex had not unsheathed her sword yet. The steward reeled around, furious with his failed attempt, he cursed at Alex.

"I'm going to feed your bones to the dogs." Lunging at Alex again, his sword sliced towards her head. Alex at that instant deftly sidestepped, parrying the mighty blow with her now drawn sword as she maneuvered behind Braunn's larger frame. To Braunn, Alex had vanished in front of him, until he heard the outlander's voice from behind his back.

"You'll have to do better than that!" It was now Alex's turn to speak.

"You are a blight on the face of this realm and I'm going to enjoy ridding this world of your foul existence!"

Alex moved out into the corridor to get Braunn away from Jade, the steward followed, taunting Alex as he moved forward. "When you're gone and she's mine," he pointed back at the room, "I will use her then give her to my men to do what they want with what's left."

Alex didn't rise to the bait, but she did stop moving back, lowering her weight in anticipation of her opponent's attack. As predicted, Braunn launched a blow at Alex's neck. Alex stepped towards his attack, ducked under it, and at the same time cutting with her sword, ripping into her foe's side. He roared with pain; not hadn't expecting that attack. Clutching his side, he took a few steps back to gather his thoughts on how to proceed. At that moment, one of Braunn's men appeared and immediately ran at Alex.

Her new assailant was younger and faster, but his first attack was his last. He swung wildly at Alex's head, who let the attack come in before deftly cross-stepping to her right. Then in a half circular motion, she laid her own sword on top of her attacker's and used the young warrior's arms as a guide to run her blade forward, slicing through the neck of her unfortunate foe. By this time, Braunn had closed the distance between them. Alex caught the movement late and received a glancing blow to remind her. She ignored the flesh wound and was back in the fight.

They sized each other up. Braunn had shaken off the effects of the ale and was now fully ready for combat. Alex kept low whilst working on her breathing.

"Was that your first kill, outlander? Feeling sick? You should be, he was just a boy."

His words meant nothing to Alex. Yes, it was her first kill, but not the first time she'd confronted death. The mountains had taught her that. Instead, she patiently waited on the older man's next move, and she didn't have to wait long. Braunn toppled a six-foot iron candle holder to throw Alex's guard, but it didn't work. At that moment, Jade called out to Alex, Braunn made a move for the room. Alex got there first. "Over my dead body!" Alex's tone was cold. Braunn's reply was similar in feeling.

"I'll try to oblige you." Alex stood in the doorway and dropped the tip of her Katana, which was now pointing at the floor. In effect, she was daring him to make a move.

Both were locked in concentration, not blinking. Alex kept her breathing low, relaxing every muscle possible and just keeping enough tension in the rest to retain her posture. Braunn attacked with a straight thrust. In reply, Alex moved to the left, rolling her sword edge up as she dropped to one knee. Alex's sword ran along his blade then buried itself in the tyrant's abdomen as he lunged forward. Braunn let out a gasp then a roar as Alex stood up, spilling his foe's intestines across the corridor. Alex flicked most of the blood and gore from her blade, the rest she cleaned with a small cloth from the room, then re-sheathed her weapon.

Jade had witnessed it all and sat on the bed quietly waiting for Alex to come to her. She did, sitting on the edge of the bed as she put her sword down and looked Jade in the eye. "He left me no other option." Taking Alex's hand, Jade looked at the woman she had come to love.

"There was nothing else that you could have done, Alex, he chose his path." At that moment, Tealuk came to the door.

He had seen his uncle's corpse lying in the corridor and had said a silent prayer, sending his kin's spirit to the other side in the hope that there he would find peace.

"Are you hurt, my friend?" Tealuk inquired, noticing the blood on Alex's side.

"Just a nick." Alex tried to force a smile but failed.

"You have done my people a great service. Braunn didn't earn the position of ruler, he stole it, and now that greed has cost him his life."

Tealuk's words were cold comfort for how Alex felt. Things had taken their natural course, but it was not making taking a life any easier. Jade gave Alex a little squeeze of support. Tealuk then told them the news that his father had woken up; he was weak but getting stronger. All of those gathered gave Tealuk their best wishes for his father's recovery. Kas, Finn and Asdrin then appeared at the door, looking at the carnage before the others filled them in on recent events. There was support for Alex and Jade with congratulations for Tealuk. It was then that Asdrin let out a large roar.

Everyone turned just in time to see Braunn's blade burst through the warrior's leather breastplate. Jade leaped to her feet and buried her dagger deep in Braunn's flesh. Braunn fell back to the floor dead, his face buried in a pool of his own filth. Kas lunged forward, grabbing his brother in his arms. He gently put Asdrin on the floor then stepped into the doorway, drew his sword, and took the head off the man who they had all thought was already dead. As Kas knelt next to Asdrin, he knew this would be their last words.

"Lie still, brother, the sword has cut deeply into you." There was an audible tremble in the proud warrior's voice.

"Kas, I knew that you would make a better king than me, my only wish… isss…" He was slipping to the other side. "That youuu remember me as I was, not as I am nooow…"

His words tailed off with his last breath.

Kas held Asdrin tightly and whispered in his ear the prayer that would send his brother's soul to the halls of their ancestors. They all sat quietly for a time, eventually leaving one by one to let Kas grieve in the company of his warrior kin.

Chapter Twenty-One

Some customs were respected in all the realms and this one was no different. Asdrin's body had been prepared and laid on the massive funeral pyre. By this time, Tealuk's father Rahan had summoned enough strength to attend the ceremony. There had been a purge of all the warriors loyal to Braunn; those that were left stood as honour guards on this saddest of days. What was left of Braunn's body was cast outside the Keep for all manner of scavengers to defile his corpse. This punishment was only reserved for the worst of criminals who would not join his ancestors in the next life as they had lost all honour.

Tealuk stood by his father's side; there was no joy in his face. The Uddon had lost a fellow warrior in Asdrin and although he was not of this realm, his valour was looked on with the same pride as if he were born to this kingdom. The king rose to his feet, showing his people that his strength was returning but also to stand with his fellow warriors and pay homage to one so brave. Tealuk fetched a wooden torch for the king who then stepped forward to a small fire set to the side of the main pyre. Before lighting the torch, he spoke to those gathered. "Friends, family and fellow warriors, we stand here today to honour our fallen kinsman but also to make a solemn promise that never again will we allow ourselves to be blinded and made complacent by power and greed." Kas looked at the king who caught his eye. "This man has lost his only brother because we lost our way. It is a heavy burden for us all to bear but especially hard for me that he died so bravely so that we all could live free."

Kas could no longer hold back his emotion and openly wept for his fallen kin. Jade move to his side and put her arm around him. He nodded a thank you then they lifted their gaze to the top of the pyre where Asdrin's corpse lay waiting for its journey ahead. The power of the king's words rang out across the Keep's main courtyard and soared over the battlements; no one struggled to hear him. "I pass this torch to Kas, son of Gorran, so that he may send Asdrin's spirit to the other side, to the hall of all the warriors who have passed over to continue their journey onward." Kas stepped forward and took the torch from the king, then Rahan did something unexpected; he embraced Kas and whispered in his ear. "Death is only the beginning. Your brother's sacrifice is a gift that shall be retold for centuries to come. In that, he will never truly be dead." The king tightened his embrace and looked into Kas' eyes.

To Kas, it was as if he were looking into his own father's eyes, so much so that his next words were, "Thank you, father." The king smiled and stepped backwards to stand by Tealuk. Kas lit the torch. Before placing it on the fire, he said the words that would beckon his brother's spirit to the world beyond.

"In this life of light, you walked the warrior path. Now that your spirit is free, may it forever travel in peace with our forebears."

After Kas had lit the fire, the rest of those close to Asdrin lit their torches then threw them, as was tradition, into the flames. As the pyre fuelled with oil took hold, everyone stood back to pay their last respects to a fallen warrior. One by one, they left in silence till only Kas remained. He would stay with his brother and fast till the sun returned the next morning, as was their tradition. There would be no feast to honour the dead. Under the circumstances, the king felt that quiet reflection was a better way to remind his people of the events that had led to Asdrin's untimely death.

The Keep was silent till the next morning. Kas' friends looked out, all they could see of him and Faldor were their silhouettes set against the embers of the dying fire.

Chapter Twenty-Two

As a scientific centre, CERN was massive. The main complex and ancillary structure would make up the size of a small town. The Large Hadron Collider itself was housed deep underground, mostly for safety reasons, and consisted of a twenty-seven-kilometre ring of the main particle accelerator. The rings themselves were housed inside coiled super-conducting electron magnets cooled with liquid helium down to -271.3 degrees, colder than deep space. Opposing magnets bent and shaped the beams that ran inside the ultra-high vacuum, allowing particles to accelerate close to the speed of light. At this point, they could be directed to one of four collision chambers, Atlas being the largest. All these experiments were watched over by the CERN Control Centre where each of the technical infrastructure and services that governed all scientific endeavors could be found.

Standing in this control room, Tom Johansen felt like a god. He loved the buzz of activity prior to an experiment and very soon it would be his turn. The room itself reminded him of the time he had spent at NASA whilst studying for his PhD; banks of monitors, computers lights flashing here and there, and scientists adorned with headsets ticking off a well-choreographed checklist. But at this moment, he was babysitting some VIPs as a favour to Director Grearson. Whilst performing this chore, he was working on how to execute his plan to take over the control room.

Over the last few months, Tom had been making a small arsenal of different devices; smoke and pipe bombs, percussion grenades, and he had even purchased on the dark net a Glock 9mm handgun. He had managed to conceal all these weapons and get them on site. They were now hidden behind the plasterboard wall in his room, knowing that security never checked the rooms. "Professor Johansen is there any chance of the collider being as dangerous as everyone thinks?" The voice seemed so far away but immediately brought Tom back from his thoughts. He replied to the question.

"If it was as dangerous as some people think, then I for one would not be standing here." A broad smile rippled across Tom's face. "Is everyone ready for some food?" His captive audience nodded in unison.

Later that night as Tom slept, he was held in the grasp of his latest vision. In his dream there were scenes of destruction, cities laid to waste, the dead and dying strewn everywhere. It was as if the Bible prophecies had been let loose upon the earth. Tom stood above from his mountain vantage point, the good professor laughing insanely at the picture before him. Every now and then, he would stop laughing and whisper, "You wouldn't listen, but I told you, I told youuu…" Then the laughing began again.

Tears of joy ran down Tom's face then fell, turning to blood before hitting the ground around his feet. He stood in a pool of his own blood laughing at the rebirth of this new world.

Chapter Twenty-Three

Alex woke, her first thoughts were for Kas. She dressed, leaving Jade to sleep on. Making her way to the main courtyard, she found Kas still standing guard over what remained of the funeral pyre. Alex stood for a moment before approaching her friend. When she got close enough, she reached out her hand and placed it gently on Kas' shoulder. Kas turned to Alex and greeted her with tired eyes. "It should have been me who was put to the flame!" Kas paused, looking at the ashes that stirred every now and then in the morning breeze.

He continued, "Asdrin was supposed to return home and one day lead our people as father had done before him. Now this." Again, he focused his gaze at the scorched ground in front of both men.

Alex took Kas by the shoulders, purposely turning him away from his brother's final resting place. Alex spoke in a sympathetic tone.

"Asdrin died a warrior's death and that had been written there for him in time itself. You, my friend, are a born leader of your people and the best way you can honour your brother is by living life till your time comes to join your ancestors." Kas looked at Alex through sad eyes and nodded.

"You're right, my friend, you're right," he whispered with a sense of reluctance, "It's what he would want, it's what my father would want." At that, Kas pulled a small leather pouch out of his inner pocket then walked to the remains of the fire, placing a handful of ashes inside. He returned to Alex's side. "I will bury these ashes when we return home; that way, a part of him will remain with his people." Alex nodded in agreement then the two friends walked slowly back to the Keep.

Faldor's internal systems had gone into overload. He was restless and confused, panting heavily. He let out a howl, then another and another. This drew the attention of everyone within earshot, including Kas. When Kas got to where Faldor was sitting, the dog seemed to settle. "What's wrong, my friend?" Kas took the dog out of the Keep and down to the shoreline near to where the ships were moored. Faldor kept looking over his shoulder, back in the direction from where they had come.

In the skies above them, Storm was suffering the same symptoms as Faldor. He had flown out of the Keep without Tealuk's permission, which had never happened before. At that moment, he'd seen to his father's needs and was returning to his own room. On entering his quarters, he immediately knew something was out of place and stepped backwards outside, thinking to himself, 'Where's Storm?'

Alex woke up as Jade kissed her eyelids. "Good morning!" she said and took in Jade's radiant beauty. They embraced for a while longer before Alex leapt from the bed.

"I'm going to get a quick wash then check on Kas." Jade spoke to Alex's back.

"It's really hit him hard. I know if it were my brother, I'd be inconsolable." She nodded her agreement.

Jade got out of bed and began to dress. Alex had finished washing and was drying herself when she noticed a ripple on the surface of the water she had just used. The ripples got bigger with each passing second.

"Jade, let's get out of here, NOW." There was fear in her voice. They ran out of the room and met Finn in the hallway, bits of masonry falling everywhere as they headed for the main courtyard.

Just as they got outside, all hell broke loose. There was a massive earth tremor that made it difficult to walk let alone run. Alex found an open space where she thought they would be safe. Tealuk had run to get his father the moment the earth had shook and had got halfway there when he was met by both his father and his attendants. Candlesticks and flags that hung on the wall fell to the ground. He ushered them quickly back the way he had come and joined Alex and Jade in the middle of the square. Alex checked the others then inquired about Kas. "It all happened so fast that I didn't get a chance to see if he got out." Tealuk looked at the faces of the others, but no one had seen Kas.

Kas and Faldor were in trouble. They had been on the shoreline when the quake started. As the tremor had intensified, one of the small inland scull boats that was balled up on the beach began to sink into the sand. If Alex had been there, she would have told Kas it was a process called liquefaction, which happened when unstable soil was shaken and water was forced to the surface, turning the area into one giant quicksand belt. To Kas, this looked like the work of an evil sorcerer. He called on Faldor and ran for some nearby rocks that had not sunk into the ground.

The tremor stopped as quickly as it had begun. The inside of the Keep looked like a giant had put his hands on the walls and shaken it violently. Everyone took stock of their situation, Alex, Tealuk and Jade went looking for Kas. Tealuk heard a loud screech as Storm flew down and landed on his arm. "You, my friend, were in the right place and I'm glad you're safe." Secretly Tealuk had been worried about his feathered companion.

The rescue party found Kas and Faldor sitting on the rocks where they had run to when the ground destabilized; they were glad their friends had found a safe place to sit out the quake. Alex walked towards Kas, she noticed the end of the boat sticking out of the sand and immediately knew why Kas was sitting on the rocks. "You picked a good place to rest!" There was more than a hint of sarcasm in Alex's voice, which Kas did not miss.

As the group walked back to the Keep, they let Kas know that no one had been hurt in the quake, just a few cuts and bruises. They neared the outer walls of the Keep when Alex took a hold of Tealuk's arm. "Ready your people to leave immediately!" She said.

Tealuk turned to talk to Alex, but his friend's eyes were focused on the volcano beyond the Keep. "What is it, Alex?" There was worry in the young warrior's voice and what Alex told him next only increased it.

"Do you see the east ridge?" She pointed up the mountain. At this moment, everyone was looking to where Alex had drawn Tealuk's attention. "Do you see that depression with a small dome in the middle?" The group responded, "Yes." "That's all new, the dome is the start of the magma chamber rising." Only Jade really understood what she was saying. Alex continued. "Magma is basically molten rock, rock that is so hot, it is liquid like you have in the caverns here. The magma is formed deep underground but can escape to the surface if placed under extreme pressure." She looked at their faces. "The tremors we have been feeling is the magma forcing its way to the surface. The closer it gets, the more severe the tremors become." Alex continued her lecture. "Usually volcanoes erupt vertically, up." She demonstrated using her hand to mimic an explosion. "What I'm seeing here reminds me of a similar volcano that I studied called Mount St Helens. This type of volcano is slightly different because it erupted to the side." Again, she used her hand in a similar fashion as she'd done before. Jade was holding Alex's gaze.

"How long do we have?" she asked.

"How long is a piece of string? At the most, a day." Tealuk could tell that Alex was worried.

"I need to speak with my father, then we will talk to the people." Alex nodded her agreement.

In the main square people were gathered, dazed, doing what they could to help one another. At the far end of the square Tealuk could see his father. He was being attended to as usual by his oldest and most loyal men. The old man's eyes met those of his son. "I will not leave; this is my home!" Tealuk was always amazed at how his father had the ability to read his thought processes.

"If this is your wish, I will not try to change the mind of my king. I must ask for your permission to talk to our people, see if there are any among them that want to leave our now doomed homelands." Tealuk's eyes never wavered and neither did his father's. They both knew they were doing the right thing in their own way. When Rahan spoke, there was resignation in his words.

"You are now king to our people. Their future lies in the decisions that you now make, their fate is in your hands now." The old man smiled; he knew that he'd made a good choice in how prepared his son was for this day.

Tealuk looked down at his father, his king. He was so proud of his father's courage and honour. He always knew this day would come but not under these circumstances. Tears rolled down the young man's face and onto the hand of his father's, which now cradled his cheek. After what seemed like a lifetime, they stood up and moved to the centre of the courtyard to address their people.

"The mountain is going to be destroyed the next time the ground shakes. We need to leave. My father, your king, has chosen to stay." Tealuk never told the people that his father had made him their king. He thought that duty belonged to the king alone. Rahan mustered all his strength and got to his feet. He knew he was dying but kept it from Tealuk.

"My people, my kin, the words my son has spoken are true. This place that is our home will vanish beneath the mountain. I have chosen to stay, and I have also given my title to Tealuk, my son, who is now your leader, your king!" There was great power in Rahan's voice and words. "You must leave this place and start afresh in a land of your new king's choosing. There you will rebuild a better home for you and your king." In the main square there was a lot of emotion. People were crying, others shouting Rahan's name, while some were still dazed from the recent events. Tealuk let the noise die down.

"Those wishing to leave take only what you need for the journey ahead. Anyone choosing to stay, you have our blessings. May the ancestors watch over you."

Alex accompanied by Jade had gathered their belongings when they were summoned by the old king. Tealuk stood by his father's side; they had already said their goodbyes but there was one last thing Rahan needed to do before they left. Alex stepped forward at the king's beckoning. "My dear girl, our realm owes you so much!" Alex tried to speak but the king gestured with his hand. "I see in you a warrior to match the one standing by my side." Rahan looked into Tealuk's eyes. He could see there were tears running down his son's face, as there were on his. "It would be my wish to watch you grow old together, but time and fate have caught up with these old bones." Alex and Jade stood with tears meandering down their cheeks. "I do have one last official task to complete." Rahan asked his oldest and dearest attendant to bring forward the metal box he was holding.

The king placed his hands beneath his collar and fished out a key. He lifted the cord over his head and put the key into the elaborately worked metal box; with a snap, the box was opened. Inside there was a small metal cylinder, which the king took out and kept in his hand. He thanked the attendant then turned his attention back to Alex. "These have been the ruin of all that have held them and may still be the ruin of us. They match the one on you have." He pointed to Alex's amulet. "You know what needs to be done. It is not an easy task, one with great peril, but I can see in you the future of all the peoples of the realms. You are a guardian of light. Banish this Darkness to the pit from whence he came!"

He handed Alex the cylinder. Alex then took the box with one hand and gently held the king's hand with the other. They locked eyes for the briefest of moments before the old man smiled, putting Alex's spirit at rest.

In their rooms, Kas and Finn were gathering their belongings before leaving the Keep for the last time. As they walked to join the others, Kas asked Finn a question. "Can't you use your gift to stop this?" Finn's answer was simple.

"My people work with nature, not against it. There is no force alive that could contain the raw power about to be unleashed." For a moment, Kas was silent. His next suggestion sent a cold shiver down Finn's back.

"What about Alex's charm?" Finn stopped what he was doing. He placed both hands on Kas' shoulders and looked him square in the eyes.

"We can't ask that of Alex, it would be the end of everything!" His friend's words seemed to snap Kas back into the moment.

"I don't know why I said that!" His words tailed off.

"Now Alex has all the pieces together she, we, are all in grave danger. The Darkness knows this and will look for weaknesses in us all. We must look out for each other, even more than we already have."

On the boats, everyone had stowed away their meager belongings. Kas and the others including Faldor and Storm were on Tealuk's own ship, which he had helped to build. The new king gave the order for the rowers to make way, the massive oak oars cutting through the water with a metronomic precision. Alex had been quiet since boarding and Jade knew she was in deep thought. They were halfway down the fjord when the volcano erupted. As Alex had predicted, it was one, massive, and two, a horizontal blast. Everyone looked back towards the Keep, they could observe a strange small wave pursuing their vessels getting closer and closer. Alex shouted to everyone, "Get down!" and they all complied. Just in time, the blast wave that hit the boats was immense but luckily no one was injured. Alex moved forward to talk to Tealuk.

"We need to make sail!" Tealuk was perplexed.

"Alex, we row out to the ocean and set sail." Alex grabbed the king's arm firmly and looked back. There was a curtain of ash moving out from the volcano and heading straight for the Keep. It was a pyro-plastic flow, super-heated gas with rocks and ash.

"When the landslide hits the water, it will send up a wave." Tealuk had heard of this. "The flow will ride across the surface of the water, pushing a cushion of hot air in front of it, which hopefully will propel us out of danger!" They men made sail.

The great flow devoured the Keep like an angry dragon let loose on the mountain side. Now it turned its attention on the fjord. Everyone on the ships saw the devastation reaped on their home. There was screaming, sobbing and looks of disbelief. As it hit the valley floor, the volume of debris crashed into the water, hissing, and exploding as it went. The force of the impact, as Alex predicted, threw up a massive wave.

The beast rode the crest of the wave, billowing out steam and flames all along the top edge of the massive volume of water.

Tealuk shouted to his crew to haul their oars. He had put two of them on the rudder; the plan was that these men would hopefully use the power of the wave and the flow to steer their way out to sea. The closer the flow got, the more it felt like the underworld had been unleashed on them. Some people had jumped overboard in a vain attempt to save themselves, leaving the others to watch in horror as the great beast swallowed them, never to be seen again. The group of friends sat in the middle of the boat. Kas was first to speak.

"If we survive this, what tales we will have to tell!" He licked his lips and reached for some water. Finn spoke next.

"Most people fear my kind, but you have accepted me as an equal. For that I thank you all." Tealuk tried to speak but was lost at the passing of his father and kinsmen. Alex looked to Jade.

"I can't find the words to explain how much you mean to…" Jade reached across with both her hands and pulled her close, she kissed her lovingly as she did.

"Alex McDonald, I love you with every part of my being and if we make it out of this alive, I want to spend the rest of my life with you." She had to shout the last part of her sentence as the beast was now upon them. The massive wave started to pull them backwards into its void and just as all seemed lost, a hot blast of air inflated the sails and started to push the ships forward.

"It's working, Alex, it's working!" Tealuk had broken his silence and stood by the main mast of the ship, laughing. "You shall not have us this day, beast. We are meant for greater things!" The others pleaded with him to sit down with them, but he kept his arm wrapped around the mast. The great beast vomited the ships out of the fjord into the open ocean without any further loss of life.

The ships sat in the calm water, Tealuk's people hailed him as their saviour. The new king reached out his open hand to Alex, which he took with a firm hold. "This is our savior, not me." Tealuk joined his people in praising his friend. They sailed further along the coast and made temporary camp to tend to any injured and eat. Tealuk caught Alex's attention and the two friends moved away from the others. "Alex, is it time for you to return to your homeland?" Alex nodded.

"We will have to find a way around the volcano to get to the realm key." At this point, Tealuk whispered to her.

"There is another way for you to get home." He told Alex there was a second master key room a day's sail from their current position. Alex was stunned and excited.

They stood on the shore saying their goodbyes, Alex, Jade, and Kas were talking to Finn, who had decided to stay and help Tealuk rebuild what he and his people had lost in the eruption. "I feel this is the right thing to do and Tealuk has offered me a home, a new beginning for me." Finn's face was beaming as he spoke.

"I know we are all glad for you, our friend." Alex spoke for everyone, who then took it in turns to embrace Finn before they got on the ship. Kas asked Finn to take care of Faldor till he returned as Alex had asked Kas to help her finish this perilous task. Kas didn't hesitate to help his friend, who had become more of a sister to him.

The ship left the shore, Tealuk's people sung a traditional song to say farewell to loved ones and to wish them luck on the voyage ahead. The mood on the ship was somber as they sat thinking about what had come to pass and what had yet to come in the days ahead. The noise of the waves had a hypnotic rhythm; soon all on board, save the crew, were fast asleep. Storm circled above the ship keeping a watchful eye on any potential dangers. On the boat, however, Alex was under attack.

Chapter Twenty-Four

Jade was dead. Alex's world lay in tatters. She sat with Jade's crumpled body in her arms and sobbed uncontrollably. On the other side of the key room, Kas' throat was slit and Tealuk's body lay propped partially against the furthest wall, with Alex's Katana buried deep in his torso.

Earlier they had made their way to a small island east of the mainland. They had all slept through most of the journey, exhausted from the rigours of their near-death experience. Sailing into a small cove, they beached the ship and Tealuk asked his men to get a fire started as the friends found the small staircase that led to the key room. The group climbed the stairs with lots of laughter as each enjoyed the others' company.

Set into an overhang in the rock was the key room, the stone carved in the same fashion as they had seen at the Keep. They entered, Tealuk asked Alex to light the torch with his trusty spark stick. Alex caught the movement late, but Kas didn't see it at all. Tealuk's sword ripped through the front part of Kas' throat, severing his carotid artery, and sending jets of blood spurting across the room. Tealuk then turned his attention to Jade. He looked her straight in the eyes; his only words to her were, "I'm sorry!"

Alex screamed her name. "JADE..." Her Katana was now drawn. "No, no, no, no!" She couldn't believe this. Alex's thoughts were interrupted by Tealuk's voice.

"You brought the power back to its rightful place, Alex. Now I have them all!" Alex stood numbed by the words coming from her friend's mouth. Tealuk continued. "My people have suffered enough. I will build them a kingdom that will rule over the other realms. YOU will bow to my will." Tealuk embraced Jade and pushed his sword through her abdomen. It was so violent a penetration that the sword erupted out of the back of her bodice right in front of Alex's eyeline. Tealuk discarded Jade's body to the side without emotion. The two fought their blades, sending sparks flashing everywhere.

"Alex, come back to me, Alex, please my love, come back to me…"

Alex and Tealuk were locked together in a mental embrace and the only noise Alex could make was a guttural scream. Tealuk continued to laugh insanely until Alex stuck her thumb into Tealuk's eye socket. The warriors now separated; Alex took her chance. She gave Tealuk a large target to attack by dropping the tip of her Katana. The man she thought was once a friend attacked with a straight thrust to Alex's unprotected torso. Alex slipped to the side and brought the back of her katana down on Tealuk's blade, the blow from the Katana shattering Tealuk's sword as he stood defenseless. Pivoting then raising his sword overhead, Alex buried it deep into Tealuk's midsection. Immediately, Alex ran to Jade and held her lifeless body close to her, she wept.

"Alex, come back to me, come back to me NOW."

Alex looked down at Jade's body. There was no life in it, but she could hear her voice and now the others. Then there was darkness.

Alex was woken by the piercing sound of a bird; a bird of prey, to be precise. She opened her eyes and saw Jade's beautiful face. She was saying something she couldn't quite hear. Raising up, Alex held Jade as if she'd been gone for a thousand years. "We almost lost you, my darling. You were under some sort of enchantment." Jade told her.

Looking over her head, Alex could see the concerned faces of her friends. Tealuk was standing with Storm perched on the gauntlet of his right arm. Alex smiled.

After eating, Alex told the others of the terrifying vision she had had. They all sat in silence for a moment until Kas spoke.

"More than ever, we must look after each other!" They all nodded in agreement. Kas continued. "Now the amulets are back together as one, we must not let our guards drop!" Again, everyone agreed.

One of Tealuk's men called him forward. When he came back, he told the others that they were coming up to land on the island. Tealuk suggested to Alex that, in light of things, maybe he should stay on the ship with his men while she, Jade and Kas climbed to the key room. Alex put an arm around her friend. "You will do nothing of the sort. We still have to say goodbye."

As before, they sailed into the cove and beached the ship and, as before, they climbed the stairs, this time in silence. The strange thing was that everything was exactly as Alex had seen in her vision. The friends entered the room, Alex lit the torch and that is where the similarities ended. They took it in turn to embrace Tealuk and thank him for all that he had done. Tealuk spoke to the group. "My friends, I hope this will not be the last time I see you. My wish for you is to complete the quest and rid our realms of this hideous harbinger of evil forever!" Alex stepped forward and slipped the Katana from her belt.

"This has been with me for many years and as you have seen, it has served me well. It is the only gift worth giving a warrior of your standing." Alex held out the sword which Tealuk accepted reluctantly.

"I have no words, my friend!" Tealuk spoke but was looking at the sword.

"None are needed." Alex took out her grandfather's watch and placed it in the appropriate slot then took Jade's hand, who in turn took Kas'.

"Goodbye, my frie…" The world went out of focus then dark as it had done before.

Chapter Twenty-Five

It was cold. Alex's party were caught in a blizzard on their side of the gate. To get out of the chill, the friends huddled on the downwind side of the massive boulder. "We need to get down as quick as we can," Alex shouted, "Kas, you are in the middle, Jade will look out for you, stay close to me." The others agreed.

Alex took the lead with Kas and Jade following her. Even though the weather was atrocious, they manage to make good time. The lower they descended, the more the snow gradually turned to rain. It took about one hour and thirty minutes before they got to the refuge of the cottage. Alex filled a warm bath of water while Jade got a fire going.

After fetching some towels from the bedroom cupboard, Alex gave one to each person. Jade was first in the bath, then Kas and finally Alex. As each took their turn to get warm, fresh clothes were waiting for them when they were dry. Jade had no spare clothes in the cottage but luckily Alex had an old pair of pajamas and one of her t-shirts. She didn't care if it kept her warm. Kas managed to borrow some of Alex's clothes, although they were a bit tight. Alex suggested a trip to Fort William for some clothes and any other supplies they needed. The cottage was in fact a good place to introduce Kas to modern mod-cons. He played with the light switch, much to the amusement of Alex and Jade.

Following an uneventful night's sleep, they rose early and left the cottage having agreed to have breakfast in the tearoom. They sat in Alex's trusty four-by-four, which to Kas was a marvel or witchcraft. When they hit the main road, he covered his eyes till the beast stopped outside of Jade's house where she quickly changed and return to the pick-up. Alex promised to drive slowly on the way to the tearoom where they would have breakfast.

Alex entered the shop, the owner Angus exclaimed, "You're alive then! You and Jade Keegan!" He pointed to the poster on the wall with the headline 'Missing Climbers'.

"Sorry Angus, but it was a spur of the moment trip." She told a version of the truth.

Jade and Kas entered the cafe to order breakfast while Alex went to explain herself to the local police and her mountain rescue colleagues. She had a stern talking to from both police and his mountaineering friends, with "bloody idiots" as a common theme.

After the grilling, Alex phoned the office and extended her annual leave period, which they agreed to as she usually overworked and was often forced to take time off. When she got back to the tearoom Jade had ordered them a full breakfast that was nearly cold, but she ate it anyway.

Kas lightened the mood. "I could get used to this!" he said, rubbing his stomach with a broad grin on his face. Alex nearly drowned poor Jade with a mouthful of lukewarm tea. Everyone was laughing except Jade, who had gone to fetch some napkins to dry herself off with.

On her return to the table, Alex apologized. They ordered some more tea and worked out a schedule for the day, returning to the cottage long enough for Alex to lock the cylinder in her grandfather's chest and place it back in the attic. Then they were off to Fort William for a wardrobe of clothes for Kas, who saw nothing of the beautiful countryside as he buried his head under a jacket on the back seat of the car. "You're just going to have to deal with it, Kas, this is how we travel most of the time." Alex's words were met with a grunt of derision.

Fort William, originally called Inverlochy, was set on the

shores of Loch Linnhe, one of Scotland's longest sea lochs. It fed the Caledonian Canal at its southern most point and had become a popular tourist destination for climbers and extreme sports enthusiasts. Alex drove into the public car park, paid for a two hour stay, then along with Jade and Kas headed for the heart of the small historic town. They walked up one of the cobbled side roads that led to Main Street. There was a mixture of shops, pubs, cafes, hotels and B&Bs, and at the north end was a beautifully maintained village green. Jade took over at this point. "I'll be your personal shopper and stylist." As she spoke, there was laughter in her voice. Alex loved when she did this.

"I'll meet you at the pub," she pointed to the ferry bar, "In thirty minutes." Jade nodded then ushered Kas to speed up.

Alex needed razor blades. She had a fair bit of growth on her legs, and it needed to come off; it felt like a thousand ants were biting her when she walked. She found a pharmacy and bought the blades she needed. The town was busy today with people taking photographs, the hustle and bustle of a tourist hot spot. After she had done a bit of window shopping, blending in with the tourists, Alex found herself in the newsagents leafing through the glossy magazines. Not knowing why, she flicked through the pages of a few science monthlies when the answer she had been looking for was in front of her. Taking the magazine, she headed for the checkout where she paid for it then made her way to the pub to show the others what she'd found.

Kas sat resplendent in his new ensemble, looking quite pleased with himself. Between him and Jade there were a few other carrier bags full of the rest of Kas' wardrobe and a few items Jade had bought. "I'm glad I didn't give you an hour!" Alex said, looking down at the bags then back up at Jade.

"Can I shop or can I shop!"

She sat down at the table, pulled out a copy of 'Science Monthly', which as the title stated was for boffins and geeks to catch up on the latest events in the scientific community. Jade looked at Alex.

"Is this the result of your thirty minutes shop? Because I'm not impressed." Alex fished out her razors and raised her eyebrows mockingly. They laughed at each other again. Their attention turned back to the magazine and its cover shot, which read, 'When Worlds Collide; An exposé on eminent physicist, Prof. Thomas Johansen.' There was a picture of the good professor circled by a mockup of the Large Hadron Collider.

After a moment, Jade exclaimed, "Is he a friend of yours, *prof*?" She poked fun at Alex, and she laughed.

"I broke a rib there. You're hysterical, I have told you that." They laughed. "Seriously, I've seen this guy before somewhere and I've found a place to get rid of the talismans." Jade was quiet for about a minute and when she spoke again, there was no humour in her tone.

"Firstly, where have you seen him? Secondly and most importantly, how are you going to get to play with the collider?" Alex sat with a furrowed brow before she finally spoke, telling them where she'd seen the good professor.

"I saw him when I was having the vision on Tealuk's boat." Kas looked at Alex.

"Your paths must be intertwined, my friend. I have heard of such things in my realm and always there were dark forces involved." His friend's statement brought Alex no comfort and none for Jade either. To help her block out her previous train of thought, Alex moved on to Jade's second point of order; how to get into the CERN facility. "I have a couple of colleagues that have connections that should be able to help us, and as it happens, one in particular owes me a favour."

Over an early lunch, the friends discussed a strategy or,

as Kas preferred to call it, a battle plan. Alex had given her jeweler friend a call about getting Kas some documentation. Although a reputable jeweler, Jim McLaughlin had connections in all areas and, like Alex, certain people owed him 'Favours.' Now Alex joined the list.

It was agreed they would drive south, cross to France via the Channel Tunnel, use the main motorways to get to Switzerland, then improvise from there.

"Told you it would be a piece of cake," said Alex with a roguish grin on her face. "Speaking of cake, anyone for dessert?" The others nodded, although Kas was a bit vague on what dessert was.

Once they had finished lunch, Alex took Kas to get some passport photos taken, which sounded easy but when your friend thinks putting a light switch on is some kind of sorcery, taking a picture can take some persuasion. Nevertheless, they got it done. Kas got to keep one photo, which he guarded like it was treasure, much to the amusement of his companions. Alex posted the photos first class mail and hoped Jim would receive them the next day and get the ball rolling.

Chapter Twenty-Six

Tom stood in the director's office. He looked like a schoolboy about to be reprimanded by his headmaster. Professor Grearson entered the room without acknowledging that Tom existed till he was behind his desk and sat down. "Please, Tom, take a seat. What's on your mind?" This statement got Tom thinking, 'You'll know soon enough!'

"Well?" Grearson's exclamation brought Tom back from his thoughts.

"I just wanted to thank you for your understanding of my little predicament and wondered if you would care to join me for lunch tomorrow at one of the local restaurants in town?" Paul was an astute man and immediately wondered what Johansen's play was going to be.

"That's a very kind offer, Tom, and I think it would be great to get offsite so to speak, in a less formal setting, as all colleagues should do from time to time." The director had become proficient at bending the truth to suit his purposes and on this occasion, it fitted his plans perfectly. For Tom, it was a means to an end in his grand scheme.

"Thank you so much, Director Grearson, what time?" Before Grearson could answer, Tom did it for him. "Say twelve thirty?" Paul nodded his head but was chuckling inside.

"Was that all, Tom? I've got some matters to deal with…" He said this picking up a bundle of papers off his desk.

Putting up his hands, Tom gestured he was finished and left the office with a hearty, "see you tomorrow," then let himself out, closing the door behind him.

Chapter Twenty-Seven

Everything had been arranged for their trip south. Alex had spoken to Jim McLaughlin; they had arranged to meet in Callander at the woollen mill. Jim thought that given the circumstances it would be better if they had their rendezvous out of the city, Alex agreed. Jade had booked their cross-channel tickets for the Eurostar online and they would stay overnight at a local hotel. After disembarking from the train in France, they arranged another overnight stop in the historic city of Reims then on to Switzerland the day after.

The next day, Jim McLaughlin stood outside the cafe feeding Angus the Highland bull as he waited for his friend and her travel companions. When speaking to Alex previously, he had inquired as to where they had been and did it have something to do with, as Jim so eloquently put it, "that fucking thing". Alex had said, "yes and no" and that she would talk more when they met. Jim had replied in his best Glaswegian, "aye, aw rite, James Bond", then hung up the phone.

Lost in his thoughts and Angus, Jim did not see Alex pull into the parking bay behind him. Alex motioned to Jade and Kas with her index finger, "ssshhh!", she got out quietly and began to sneak up on Jim. When she got within striking distance, Alex did her best attempt at a Sean Connery impression. "Have you got the papersssshhh, Moneypenny?" Jim nearly ended up in beside Angus.

"Jesus Christ, Alex, a nearly shit ma self!" Alex shook Jim's hand then gave him a big hug.

"Good to see you, man." Alex giggled. Jim could hear laughing in the car.

"Are these comedians wae you?" Jim pointed to the car.

"Unfortunately, yes." Alex nodded.

Everyone went inside where they got a table and ordered food. Alex introduced her friends to Jim, who gave them each a firm handshake. "Nice to meet both of you. Jade, are you Hector Keegan's wee sister?" Jade was surprised because she didn't think they had ever met before.

"Aye!" she replied. They sat enjoying each other's company and the amazing food that the cafe produced. 'Nice to have a bit of normality', Alex thought as she looked at her friends around the table. Jim made eye contact with Alex and beckoned her with a nod. Alex nodded back and both headed for the car park. They got in Jim's car and went for a short drive.

"The stuff you asked for, it's in the pocket of my seat." Alex reached behind Jim's seat and pulled out a manila envelope and opened it. Inside there was a passport, driver's license, a couple of credit cards, a fuel card and loyalty cards for well-known supermarkets. Alex put the fake IDs back in the envelope and thanked Jim. "It's none of my business, buddy, but do you need anything else? Money, a gun?" Laughing, Alex turned to her friend.

"I'm not Lara-fucking-Croft, you know, and anyway, I can't carry a gun in the car, not going through customs."

"I know that, but whit's wae aw the cloak and dagger shite?"

Without telling Jim everything, Alex told him about the amulets, what she had to do with them and where they were going. All the time Jim was looking at his friend's face for any hint of a lie, there was none.

"I knew that thing was cursed. You should destroy it, before it destroys you. Hope things work out, Alex I really do. If you need help, go to that address." They pulled into the car park and went back inside.

Jim saw his friends off and watched them drive out of sight, whispering under his breath, "Fucking pendant's gonna be the death of you, my friend." He got in his car and headed back to Glasgow.

They sat in the motorway service station, Kas looked down at the documents with his picture on them. The forger had given him the name of Kas Thorsen; ironically, Thorsen meant 'Son of Thor' in Danish. Alex explained to Kas about Thor, to which he was most pleased. Kas, like Alex, was a professor of geology. His back story was that he was assisting Alex on a project studying the effects of super volcanoes and their possible risk to the future of mankind.

After sorting out Kas' history, Alex sat looking at the documents and marveled at the wear and tear that had aged the items perfectly. Kas put the cards in a wallet that his friends had bought him and the passport he kept in the inside pocket of his jacket. Considering he hadn't been in this realm for very long, Kas had adjusted surprisingly quickly to all the modern world had to offer. Both Jade and Alex had praised him for accepting the new and embracing things as they were.

Alex and Jade shared the driving duties so they could make good time and keep on schedule. Their route south took them down the M1 motorway through Leeds, Nottingham, and Birmingham, then on towards London taking the M25, turning off onto the M20 through Maidstone, then terminating at the Eurostar. Travelling through the night gave them a good chance of avoiding any traffic issues but they would have to add time on the journey from Maidstone to their rendezvous with the Eurostar. There were always holdups in this part of the country, partly to do with the fact that the Channel Tunnel was located here.

They arrived in Maidenhead early morning and got settled into their rooms at the Premiere Inn; just the usual basic suites but well kept. Alex made sure Kas was comfortable in the room before returning to hers where she found Jade asleep. Alex found unpacked the cylinder and looked at the ornately carved metal with an ancient form of writing on all the sides; the script was beautiful in its own right, long flowing characters that Rahan had told him would help to keep the contents energy contained. However, as she held it, Alex could feel the power pulsing through her whole body.

"ALEX…" the voice shrieked. Her eyes snapped open to a scene of horror.

She was on top of Jade with her hands around her throat, Jade's eyes bulging in absolute panic. Deep inside her there was a part that enjoyed Jade's fear. She slowly released her grip and cradled Jade in his arms. "Jade, I am so sorry, I don't…" Jade's hand reached out and caressed her face.

"I know it's not you." Her words were but a whisper. "Remember when I attacked you, but it wasn't me, it was him?" Her words gave Alex no comfort. She felt lost, alone and confused. They held each other, lost in their own thoughts about how this was going to end, and whether it would claim one of them or both of their souls before its hunger could be satisfied.

The sound of the door being pounded by Kas' fist brought them out of what was a deep sleep. Alex opened the door to be greeted by her friend's smiling face.

"Are you hungry?" Kas's simple statement put a smile on not only Alex's face but also Jade's, who by now was out of bed and at her side.

"Is that all you think about, your stomach?" She said this with a smile breaking across her face.

"Yes," was his simple reply. It made them all laugh.

After a late lunch, they mulled around the town, whose history could be traced back to the Stone Age. Maidstone was situated fifty kilometres southeast of London and sat on the river Medway. The King's Head pub sat on the banks of said river, and Jade suggested they have a rest here to take in the scenery and have a break from saving the world. As it was a pleasant day, they decided to sit outside. When the drinks waiter came over, Alex asked Jade what she wanted. "Surprise me!" Alex looked up at the young man.

"D'you stock Jura whiskey?"

"Of course!"

"We'll have three please."

"Do you want them with ice?"

"No thanks, where I come from that would be a sacrilege."

While waiting for the young man to return, all three friends took in the scene in front of them. Small boats shuttled to and fro, with a couple of teams sculling along. Occasional young couples were picnicking on the banks on this late summer's day. They sat silently until the waiter returned with their drinks, thanking the young man before raising each glass. Alex toasted her friends in the traditional Scottish manner.

"Slange-ee-va; your very good health." She touched glasses with Jade and Kas, and explained to Kas that the common reply was just to say, "Slange".

Kas poured the honey-coloured liquid down his throat in one go, instantly regretting his rash decision. He coughed and spluttered as the whiskey attacked his throat. Kas' antics brought a few smiles from the other guests.

Once he had recovered, he asked Alex, "Do you clean your armour with this stuff?" Alex laughed at his description of her favourite tipple.

"You are supposed to sip, savour it, not gulp it down like the mead from your home." Kas rolled his eyes. Alex demonstrated with her drink. As the liquid rolled around her mouth, she savoured the subtle tastes of the sweet malt named after the island where it was brewed.

Coming back from her thoughts, Alex told Kas that some folk watered it down and there were others who thought that this was a sacrilege. She ordered another drink for Kas and they all toasted again. This time Kas followed Alex's instructions and now could appreciate what his friend was talking about. "It reminds me of home." There was a sense of melancholy in Jade's voice. Alex agreed and Kas nodded, knowing how they felt.

On returning to the hotel, Alex received a phone call, which she took straight away. "You did? That's one I owe you, George, thanks for pulling those strings." She hung up the phone. Alex thought back to Glencoe and how she had berated her boss for sending him on what she thought was a fool's errand, but that had led them all to this moment.

"Who was that Alex?" Jade called from the bathroom.

"It was my boss, George Davidson. He managed to get us into CERN on visitor passes, isn't that great news?" As Alex said this, she put his head round the door to speak to Jade face to face. Jade stood naked with the shower running and Alex took in every exquisite curve of her body; she was in anybody's book a thing of beauty.

"Want to wash my back, professor?" Jade teased as she let the water spill over her breasts. Alex stood there for a moment enjoying how she looked then joined her.

Kas had found the TV remote and was king of his domain. He flicked through the channels until something caught his eye. It was a movie about an American army captain sent to put down a rebellion in Japan who was then captured and joined the rebels in their honorable fight. Once the movie was finished, Kas switched off the TV and lay back, enjoying the memories of his recent viewing. He fell asleep quickly and dreamed of his homeland where his brother was still alive and where everything was as it should be. "I can bring him back…" The voice spoke the words in a whisper, then repeated them louder and more directly. "I can bring Asdrin back to you and your father, Kas. All I ask in return is your allegiance." Kas, still lost in what he thought was a dream, asked the spectral voice for his name. "I have many names. In your tongue I am an abomination, he who steals children to feast on. I am the blackest corner of your mind, I am THE DARKEST PART OF YOUR ROTTEN SOUL, I AM…" Kas' eyes flew open with the name still contaminating his thoughts. Getting up, he hurried from his room to talk to Alex about his vision.

Alex and Jade listened to Kas' story, it became very apparent that things had changed, and the Darkness was aware of their purpose. Kas had told them that he had heard its name, which was spoken in his language. They knew it as 'Grindholm' – the defiler of souls. "This goes far back into the past of my people, back to a time of wood elves before the bloodlines were split." Alex and Jade sat mesmerized by the story Kas was telling. Both had heard of elves but had thought they were a fiction in folklore. Kas continued. "Evil never dies – it changes form or name or destiny, but it never goes away. There must be balance in all worlds, this applies to both good and evil. There can never be a time that is solely good. This is why there is an ebb and flow, times that are prosperous and others of war. In times of conflict, the Grindholm grows strong, and even in times of peace, if it has expanded enough it can try to take over and shift the balance back to evil!" His words hung in the air for a moment. The friends looked at each other, absorbing their current predicament. It was Alex who broke the silence.

"We must look out for each other. He is going to try again

and again to break our will and we must stand as one to keep him at bay." The others agreed.

Having checked out late afternoon, Alex drove through the town centre and headed for the M20 that would take them to Folkestone and the Eurostar. It was a two-hour drive but finally they arrived at the terminal. Keeping to the right lane, Alex followed the signs on the overhead gantries and swiped their pre-paid tickets when necessary. Next, it was border control, and they would find out if Jim's contacts had done a good job on Kas' fake IDs. "Have a nice journey." Alex whispered a thank you to Jim and drove on. There were more overhead gantries that denoted whether you were an upper- or lower-level passenger; they were lower. Again, following the signage, they got to their ramp in perfect time to start boarding. Alex smiled inwardly at her great timing, not considering that she was cutting it fine.

They drove on and were ushered into position, it became clear that anyone with a fear of confinement should probably stick to a ferry crossing. It felt a bit like a Russian doll; people in a car, inside a train, in a tunnel that was underground and beneath the sea. It took less than an hour to get to France. As any customs checks had been completed on the British side, it was just a matter of getting out of the terminal, remembering to drive on the right, then look for the A26 and head for the city of Reims, their next stop. Motorways, whatever the country, were a means to an end; they got you from point A to B with a lot of boring asphalt in between. That was the reason the friends put a couple of stops in their journey and at this point they were on the outskirts of the city of Reims. They had booked rooms at the Holiday Inn which sat on the Rue Buirette not far from the cathedral Notre-Dame de Reims (Our Lady of Reims).

The cathedral itself was a massive structure that dominated the city skyline, with the main entrance guarded by two spires framing the large ornate circular stained-glass windows. As they drove past, all were in awe of the majesty of the building and none more so than Kas. All he could say was, "beautiful". Pulling up at the hotel, they all agreed to fit time in to visit the cathedral. On entering the hotel, which had been recently renovated, they inquired at reception about their reservation. "Ah, Ms. McDonald, yes, your rooms are ready." The girl's name tag informed them she was called Christine, She had a lovely soft French accent and her manners, along with her English, were impeccable. "I love your Scottish accent; which part are you from?" Alex told Christine she was from Glasgow but had been born in the Scottish Highlands. "You are very lucky to have been brought up in such beautiful surroundings." Alex smiled as the girl continued. "I have visited Scotland once with my friend, we went to the Cairngorms National Park, and it was so beautiful. You're a very lucky to live there."

With that, Christine called the porter and instructed him to take their luggage to the rooms designated, which were 10 and 12 on the first floor. Alex thanked Christine then they followed the porter to the elevator. After a short ride to the first floor, they arrived at their rooms and the porter showed them how to use the electronic keys and bid them good day. Alex fished out five euros and handed it to the porter, who left with a curt "merci, madam". Once again, they settled into their rooms and agreed to meet for dinner in the hotel's very own Italian restaurant.

Alex had left Jade sleeping as she departed the hotel and headed to find the city's main square. Christine had given her directions to an address, and it took her no time to find her bearings. She passed a bronze statue of Joan of Arc resplendent on her horse, then looked for the Rue de Vesle that dissected the city north to south. Alex strode purposely in a northerly direction.

Inside the envelope Jim had given her was a small package, probably more fake passports by the feel of them. There was an address in Reims that Alex had to memories. Alex had told Jim she may need a gun but didn't want to take the risk of having it till they reached France.

Alex walked farther up the Rue de Vesle till she found the address she was looking for, which as luck would have it, was a jewelers. Entering the shop, she walked up to the counter and asked to see the manager. The salesgirl went into the back of the shop and returned with a middle-aged man who told Alex his name was Henry. After the brief introduction, Alex told Henry that her friend Jim had sent her with some goods to this address. The manager ushered Alex to the back of the shop where it was more private. Alex gave him the package, which Henry put in the safe. Henry then scribbled an address on a notepad, tore it off and handed it to Alex, who put it in her pocket then shook the manager's hand and left the shop.

On the way back to the hotel, she memorized the address in Geneva then threw the scrap of paper down a drain in the road. When she got back to the room, Jade was having a cup tea. "Where have you been, madam?" There was a massive smile on her face as she teased her, again.

Alex told her she'd been for a walk and had found a statue of Joan of Arc. Jade asked if they could go there after dinner and Alex told her "Of course".

Alex knocked on Kas' door. Kas opened it with a grin on his face. "Alex, come in, come in." Alex entered the room with an air of suspicion. "Are you ready for dinne…" His last word tailed off as Alex noticed the small drinks bottles on the table.

"I see you've found the mini bar!" She pointed to the

small cabinet.

"Yes, Alex, it's very good." Again, he had that grin on his face. Alex laughed to herself, thinking she would have to watch her friend's alcohol intake at dinner.

"You ready to eat, Kas?"

"Yes, will there be cake?"

"I'm sure they will have one just for you, my friend."

They went up to the Italian restaurant and were shown to their table, which was by the window and gave them a stunning outlook over Notre-Dame de Reims. There was a lot of joy at the table as they all reveled in each other's company. After dinner, they agreed to get up early and take in the cathedral's beauty. Alex and Jade bid Kas good night then went for a stroll to see Joan of Arc.

Alex was quiet on the walk. She didn't like deceiving Jade and Kas about what was ahead in Geneva but felt he had to bear the burden of that till the time was right. Jade picked up her mood. "What's on your mind?" Alex smiled.

"Can't keep anything from you, Sherlock." This time they both laughed. "I've just been thinking about all of this." She rolled her eyes and gestured. "It's a bit overwhelming." It was a white lie, but she could live with it.

Arriving at the site, they realized it was not that far from the cathedral, which looked majestic lit up in the early evening. Likewise, Joan of Arc looked resplendent sitting on her horse, sword held high as if calling all who were present to battle. From humble beginnings, Joan had risen and at the age of only nineteen under a divine vision had led the French forces against the English army in The Hundred Years War. This had helped reclaim the throne for Charles VII who was later crowned king in Reims Cathedral and suffered all his life from insanity. Joan was captured by English forces, tried, found guilty of various charges, and burned at the stake in 1431. In 1456, Pope Callixtus III retried the case and threw out the charges then declared her a martyr. She was sainted in 1920 by Pope Benedict XV. Joan of Arc remained a pivotal and inspiring figure from history revered by the French people.

Alex had scanned the information board next to the statue and read the relevant points. She turned to Jade. "She kinda reminds me of you."

"Alex McDonald, where did that come from?" Jade took Alex's hands and kissed her. Alex continued.

"You are brave, courageous, you talk straight and you're a woman. If that's not an exact match, well, I'm…" Jade kissed Alex again, this time more passionately.

"Alex, why couldn't I have met you years ago?" Jade gazed into her eyes, and she was lost for words momentarily.

"We did meet before. I was your brother's friend." Jade linked arms with Alex and the pair walked back in the direction of the hotel. She continued the conversation.

"No, I mean, why couldn't it have been like this earlier in our lives!" Jade leaned her head against Alex's shoulder waiting for her answer.

"Karma. The Japanese believe all things are governed by this, that all things will come and go when they are meant to. It is a universal law." Jade held her tight and when she spoke, it was from the heart.

"I've been hurt, Alex, you know, before… If I had found you at an earlier point in my life, things would have been a lot different." Alex stopped, she took Jade by her shoulders and stared straight at her.

"We're here now and that's all that matters, and as an added bonus, you get to help me save the world." Jade punched Alex very hard, which took the wind away from her.

"See what happens when I drop my guard?" She wheezed. Jade was laughing at her and trying to apologize at the same time.

"Why were you so guarded?" Jade asked the question not expecting a big answer but when Alex spoke, it touched her deeply.

"I've been hurt too, Jade, and I've hurt people as well. I think some of it was to do with my parents' death, not really knowing them, I felt incomplete. That is not taking anything away from my grandparents, they were all I cared for. But there was never anyone who made me feel the way you do. It's karma that has brought us together at this moment in time."

Alex was surprised by the tears welling in the corners of her eyes. Jade's floodgates had already burst, and she was crying openly. They held each other for some time then made their way back, walking in silence, just enjoying the feeling of being more complete.

In the hotel, they lay in each other's arms and talked into the small hours, gradually falling asleep maintaining their lovers embrace. Tomorrow they would be in Geneva then on to what destiny lay in wait at CERN.

Chapter Twenty Eight

Tom was not particularly good at small talk while driving, which meant Director Grearson's journey to the restaurant was rather dull. The only points of interest for him had been crossing the river Rhone, which he fished regularly but not this far down, and watching the planes coming into land at Geneva international airport. The restaurant Au Grizzly was located only five minutes' drive from the airport at 1218 Le Grand-Saconnex. As they pulled into the carpark, they were greeted by a large sign that read 'RESTAURANT' in neon with 'THE GRIZZLY' underneath. Tom switched off the ignition and beamed.

"We're here. Hope you like steak." Grearson smiled as Tom attempted to be the gracious host.

"Of course, I do, Tom, and I've heard great things about this place."

"Good, good, good." Tom put his hand on the director's back to get him to move forward but Grearson simply had to look sideways to facilitate its removal, then he stepped forward of his own choice. Tom walked at Grearson's shoulder like a dog on a leash, only moving forward to get the external door then the internal one. Both men were greeted by a wonderful aroma.

Tom was met by the head waiter but before he could speak, Tom blurted out, "I've a reservation for two; Johansen."

"Certainly," the waiter replied as he checked down the bookings list. "This way, gentlemen." He ushered the men forward.

Inside the restaurant was like a Tudor house with dark beams and off-white walls. In contrast, the tables were covered in bright red cloths with cream napkins. The waiter seated the men at a table next to the window before taking their drinks order. Grearson spoke to the waiter first. "David, is it ok to call you by your first name?"

"It is sir."

"Great. Firstly, I must compliment you on your English, it is perfect, have you spent time in the UK or America?" Paul Grearson had a way with people and had always found that including them in the experience was rule number one. The waiter briefly looked at his feet before replying.

"I spent some time in the UK. My father worked there for a few years, so I had plenty of time to acquire the accent." Paul sat with a smile on his face as David spoke.

"Where abouts in the UK were you?"

"Kent," was David's reply.

"I thought it was in the south. That is great, David. Anyway, back to the booze. Since I won't be driving today, I'll have a Jack and soda." David turned his attention to Tom who was mesmerized by the way Grearson engaged people.

"I'll have a sparkling water, I'm the driver today." Tom tried to mimic Grearson's easy manner but failed miserably. David thanked both men and informed them that their server would be Maria, then returned to his duties.

"What a nice young man!" The Director was baiting Tom and he fell for it.

"A little too smooth for my liking, I prefer not to being engaged by the servi…"

"Your drinks, gentlemen. My name is Maria, if there is anything you need, please don't hesitate to ask. Here are your menus and the soup of the day is mushroom." Both men thanked Maria then opened their menus. Paul brought Tom back to his previous statement.

"Sorry, you were saying, Tom?"

"Er, I tend not to engage with the staff, it makes life less complicated," he lied.

Grearson, not looking up from his menu, said, "I'm sorry, Professor Johansen, but I don't agree with that. I've always found by engaging people you make a connection and I tend to find that they will do more for you." Grearson left it hanging there, looking for a bite. It didn't take long. Tom was furious.

"Well, I beg to differ with you, Paul, but we will have to agree to disagree!" Then he shoved his head back into the menu.

The director loved this little game. He kept quiet, hoping the uncomfortable silence would take its toll on Tom's psyche. After almost five minutes, which Paul thought must be some sort of record, Tom sheepishly asked him if he was having a starter. "Yes, I think the garlic bread is speaking to me, and then I think I'll have the house special, meat on a rack, flambéed." Tom nodded his approval and decided on the same meal just as Maria returned.

"Are you guys ready to order?" Maria smiled at her charges. Paul gave her their order and asked for another Jack and soda. She collected the menus and returned with the cutlery for their starter and the all-important second drink. Grearson changed the conversation.

"Not long till you get your experiment up and running." Tom seemed to grow a couple of inches on hearing this.

"Yes, yes, yes, I'm very excited, I think this will be the culmination of years of my work, my expectations are positive."

Paul Grearson sat in his chair thinking, 'self-centered little prick, I'm glad your days are numbered, best decision I have made in a long time.' The director was still caught in this train of thought when the starters arrived.

The garlic bread sat on a base of salad with its own bottle of virgin olive oil and dressing. Both Tom and Paul changed positions in their chairs so they could sit up in a straighter posture. Maria served the starters and poured them both a glass of water and bid them "bon appetite". Tom wolfed down his garlic bread but left the salad, which forced a comment from Paul.

"Hungry?" Tom was gulping down his glass of water when the director spoke and tried to answer him whilst drinking, which only caused him to have a choking fit.

"Jesus Christ, Tom, get a grip and slow down!"

Tom apologised, "I haven't eaten today."

After finishing his starter, Paul excused himself and headed for the bathroom. Tom seized the moment and poured the contents of the small vial he had brought with him containing a mild sedative into Grearson's glass. He then picked up the glass and swilled it around to blend it with the contents.

On the other side of Geneva, Alex and the others were driving to a rendezvous with one of Jim McLaughlin's contacts. They looked down Lake Geneva, the view was stunning. They were approaching one of the area's most striking features, the Jet D'eau, a giant water fountain just offshore of the city and today's meeting place. They pulled into the car park next to a small cafe called Le Jet. Alex had briefed the others about the meeting on the drive down to Geneva. Jade was cautious; she did not like guns, and she did not want Alex mixed up in any dodgy deals.

Inside Le Jet, Alex walked up to the bar and asked the bartender, "Parlez vous Anglais?"

"Oui, sorry, yes."

"Great, I'm looking for a man called Francesc." The barman pointed to the back where there was a dark-haired young man with sharp features. "Thank you," said Alex. Walking to the rear of the cafe, she left ten euros on the bar, which the barman pocketed quickly. When Alex got to the back of the cafe, there was a strong smell of marijuana coming from Francesc's direction. The young man had watched Alex come in then head in his direction. He took a last puff on his joint then hid it under the table. "Hi, are you Francesc?" Alex asked.

"Who wants to know?" Francesc had a strong Spanish accent with a touch of French mixed in; 'probably from Catalonia,' Alex thought.

Francesc continued, "You're from Glasgow?" Alex was taken aback. "I went to Glasgow University, studied veterinary medicine, left after three years, too cold." Alex stood for a moment taking in what the young man had said then sat down.

"Jim McLaughlin sent me. Do you have the package?" Francesc took out his joint and inhaled deeply.

"Why do you need a gun, my friend? Plan to rob yourself a Swiss bank?" He exhaled with a big grin breaking across his face. Alex was getting tired of this game. She pushed her position.

"Have you got the package or not?" The young man stubbed his joint on the underside of the table and pulled out a small cloth that was triangular. Alex reached over and took the cloth, putting the weighty package in her jacket pocket before bidding Francesc good day. As Alex got up from his chair, Francesc took her by the arm.

"Give my regards to Jim." Alex pulled her arm away and left the bar, nodding to the barman on her way out of the door. She had to squint against the low morning sun then walked to the car. They were just about to pull out of the car park when a police car pulled up next to them. Alex and Jade froze. Kas was lost as to what was going on but copied the others' behavior. Alex slipped the car into reverse just as the two police officers got out of theirs. The officer on the passenger side tipped the brim of his cap at Alex on getting out of the car. Alex gave him a nod, trying to look as relaxed as she could under the circumstances. Both officers disappeared into Le Jet, Alex watched in the rear-view mirror and a moment later they re-appeared with Francesc. Alex took this as her cue to leave then head out of the city.

Tom sat studying Grearson for any signs of the drug taking hold. Maria appeared with one of the chefs who pushed a serving trolley containing the main course. Everything looked fantastic and Paul said so. "Guys, this looks amazing!" Tom sat frustrated and said nothing, choosing to let Grearson speak for them both. "Well, this is a first for me, I've never been served steak in this way." Paul was referring to the meat being hung on ornate iron hangers which the chef coated with brandy and flambéed right there at the table. Once the flames had died down, the ornate hangers were left on the table for the guests to serve themselves. Paul shook the chef's hand. "Thank you so much for your time, chef, I can't wait to get started on this delicious meat." Paul gestured to the meal set before the two men. The chef bid them good day and returned to his duties. Maria had finished placing the rest of their meal then followed the chef back into the kitchen.

The director looked across the table at Tom, who had been staring at him every now and then. He wondered what his game was, so he asked him. "Have I got a piece of dirt on my face, Tom?" Grearson had caught him staring. Tom had to come up with something quickly.

"Sorry Paul, I was not staring at you," he lied again, "I was looking at the painting on the wall behind you." The director turned in his chair and looked at the landscape painting on the wall. "Looks like Colorado in the fall." Both men's attention returned to the meals, but Paul was keeping a close eye on his dinner guest. Putting his suspicions to one side for a moment, Paul passed a comment on the meal.

"This is something else. Please, Tom, don't wait on me, please tuck in." As if being given permission by his father, Tom took some meat off the hanger and put it on his plate next to the fries and mixed vegetables. He then cut a piece of meat and started to eat. The meat was perfectly done for both men and for once Tom slowed his eating down, savouring every mouthful. He still had one eye on Grearson but could not ignore the exquisite taste in his mouth or the skill in preparing it. Tom caught Grearson's eye and asked his opinion on the meal. "Well, Tom, I have to thank you for giving me one of the best eating experiences I've had in a long time." Tom could tell Grearson's words were genuine and for a split second had regrets about drugging his boss.

"Thank you very much, Paul, I had a fair idea you would like it."

The director was feeling very groggy by the end of the meal and hoped he was not coming down with anything but suspected he was. Tom looked across the table at Grearson.

"Are you ok, Paul? You look kind of grey, was it something you ate? Shall I call for the manager?" The director waved off Tom's fake concern.

"No, no, I think that I may be coming down with a cold or something." Tom asked Maria if they could have the check and she returned in under a minute with the bill. He paid by cash and unusually for him left a hefty tip. Maria thanked him.

As the men got up, Paul stumbled and was saved by a table. Tom took his arms. "Paul, let me help you." It was only at this point that the director started to feel ill at ease but felt powerless to do anything about his current situation.

By the time Tom got to the car park, Grearson was almost unconscious. Tom quickly got his boss into the passenger side of the car and clipped his seatbelt on, then calmly got into the driver's seat. His only concern was being stopped by the police, but he would have to face that problem when it arose. The idea was to keep Grearson out of the way long enough for Tom to execute his plan.

Driving back towards CERN was a nerve-wracking journey but the thoughts of his work coming to fruition helped Tom from going to pieces. He parked the car about half a mile from the facility then walked the rest of the way to Gate B and its guardhouse. As he approached the checkpoint, Tom remembered that he had left his driver's window open. It was an oversight he had not planned for and a bit late to rectify; he had to focus on the task at hand. "Good evening, Professor Johansen, where is your car?"

"Hi Bob, had a breakdown so left the rust bucket for the garage to pick up."

"What have you done with Director Grearson?" For a moment Tom thought he had been caught but realized that Bob was just making small talk.

"Director Grearson had another appointment, so I dropped him off at that and started to drive back when the car packed in." As he spoke, Tom eased the syringe of sedative out of his jacket pocket then distracted the security guard's attention by pointing at one of the monitors. "Hey Bob, what's that?" Tom pointed to the CCTV screen with his finger. As Bob turned around and looked up, Tom slipped the hypodermic needle into the guard's upper arm.

"You basta…" The anesthetic worked fast, faster even than Tom had expected.

On entering the guardhouse, Tom checked Bob's pulse, which was regular. He then slipped the keys from the unconscious man's body and stepped outside, checking no one had seen him. They had not.

Tom made his way quickly to the accommodation block, passing restaurant number one on route. On getting to his apartment door, he fished the room key out, dropping it on the floor in his haste. "Slow down, slow down," he told himself, but was very aware of the tight schedule to make his plans come to fruition. On entering the apartment, he picked his laptop off the counter and sat it on the bed. Next, Tom went to his stash of guns and pipe bombs which he placed carefully in a hold-all then on the bed. All the time Tom was doing this, a voice in his head repeated "soon, soon, soon", to which he replied out loud, "I know, master, you will be free soon!"

Alex passed a sign for the Jura mountains, which made her think of his favorite malt and, of course, of home. Kas, who had been sleeping through most of the journey, sat up and spoke to Alex.

"This man, Johansen, is he a warrior and does he have an army?" Alex smiled internally before answering Kas.

"He is a scientist, like a sorcerer, and no, he has no army save for his dark master." At the mention of dark master, Kas thought of his fallen brother Asdrin, then a wave of anger mixed with sadness came over him.

"We must destroy this sorcerer Johansen and send his vile master back to the depths of the underworld from which he was spawned." Alex and Jade almost simultaneously nodded their agreement.

At that moment, the Sat-Nav told them they were five miles from their destination. Everyone went quiet in the car. As the friends neared the CERN complex, the tension in the car was measured. They had run through the plan, and it seemed logical; the only thing left for them was to implement it. Up ahead in the distance they noticed a man in a very smart business suit stumble out of a car and head towards the facility.

Something in Alex's intuition told her to pull over and stop. The man with salt-and-pepper hair looked disheveled and groggy. Alex rolled down her window. "Do you need any help?"

"That fucking Johansen's a dead man when I catch up with him." On hearing Johansen's name, Alex understood why her gut had told her to pull over.

"Get in, we know where you're going." Director Grearson did not hesitate to get into the car. He too felt like it was the correct course of action. As Grearson sat down in the backseat, Alex made the introductions. "My name is Professor Alex McDonald; this is my partner, Jade." She nodded in the direction of their new passenger. "And the big guy sitting next to you is Kas."

"Paul Grearson, Director of the CERN facility." Alex thought this was interesting. After the brief introductions, Director Grearson continued the rant that he had started outside the car. "I don't know what that fucking maniac Johansen is up to but I can guess it is not in the interest of science." It was at this point that Alex spoke up.

"Funny you should mention Professor Johansen. We're here to see him too, and agree with you that he is up to something extremely dangerous, possibly for the whole of mankind."

"Wouldn't fucking surprise me, not after what he did to me." Paul filled them in on the day and apologized for swearing so much. The others could not believe the events that had led to the director being dumped in the car. Again, Alex seized on an opportunity.

"If there is any way we can help you, Director Grearson, you just have to ask." Paul eyed his companions for a moment before responding.

"What's your business with Johansen?" After pausing to collect her thoughts, Alex stopped the car and explained to the director.

"You know how everyone was afraid that the collider could produce a wormhole or black hole? We believe that Professor Johansen has figured out a way to do just that." Paul sat perplexed; he could not believe what he had just been told.

"The science does not add up. This was just scare mongering by Christianity and other religious fanatics." Paul's mind was racing.

"What if it's true? Could he have found a way to create an Einstein-Rosen bridge?" Einstein had theorized that the distance between two points in space could be folded to exist at the same place, making a bridge from one to the other. The downside to the theory was that it would take vast amounts of energy to create one. Paul sat quietly for the next five minutes. Finally, his focus was broken by Jade asking if he was Ok.

"Yes, yes, yes, my dear, just running the figures in my head and wondering what if…" After sitting for another moment, the director spoke again. "If you guys do not mind, could you drop me off at the nearest guard post? I need to find out where Johansen is and warn security to restrain him immediately." Alex did as the director asked and drove to the nearest guard post without asking again if he needed help.

Paul got out of the car and approached the security station. There was no one on duty and alarm bells started going off in his head. He went around to the door, which was locked. The others sat in the car wondering what to do next when they heard the director calling for Alex. As the others approached the far side of the guard post, they found Paul. "Bob should be on duty and he's not here and the door is locked. Any chance you guys could do anything about this door?" Both Alex and Kas answered, "Yes." Alex went back to the car. She opened the boot and pulled out a crowbar, then closed the boot and ran back to where she'd left the others. "Paul is it Ok for me to circumvent your security system?" Alex had a stern look on her face.

"Do it, I have a bad feeling about this."

After Alex shoved the bar between the frame and door, she asked Kas to help her put more leverage on it. The security door did its job for about a minute before succumbing to the forces exerted on it. With a large crash, the door gave way, nearly sending Alex and Kas flat on their backs. Jade and Paul rushed in only to find Bob's dead body lying on the floor of the station. Alex asked how Bob was and Jade just shook her head. Alex was enraged. "FUCKER!" She shouted. The director took off his jacket and covered his co-worker's face. As he turned to the others, he was visibly shaken to the point of crying.

"He was a good man," the director said in a shaky voice. Jade put her arms around Paul, allowing him to weep openly against her shoulder. After a moment, Paul raised his head, thanked everyone, and apologised to Jade, who in turn wiped a tear from his cheek.

"It's never easy to lose someone close." Paul nodded his agreement then turned to the others.

"Let's get this bastard." With that, the director picked up one of the spare walkie-talkies and asked for assistance; there was no reply. 'This can't be good,' he thought. Paul tried another couple of channels only to be met by static; again, he looked at the others.

"I'm afraid that something terrible is going on here." He tried the main phone line, but it was dead, then his mobile, no signal. "Damn it."

Chapter Twenty-Nine

Tom had taken out the rest of the guards who were on duty in the Meyrin campus, which was his base of operations. The killings he told himself were for 'the greater good'. On entering the main complex, he took out his MP5 machine gun, flipped the safety off and moved the selector to full auto. His plan was to empty the building by creating panic. Tom fired randomly at fire extinguishers, which exploded immediately with an ear-splitting blast, shattering windows, and blowing holes in the walls where the units were located. The effect of his actions brought people, once colleagues, into the hallways. He did not hesitate to pull the trigger, mowing them down like he was playing some virtual reality shoot 'em up. There was blood everywhere. People lay dead or near death. Tom calmly stepped over them, totally focused on the plan at hand. As he approached the main control room, there were people cowering in the hallway. Tom showed them no mercy, screaming at them, "IT'S FOR THE GREATER GOOD." Entering, one of his colleagues spoke to Tom or more pleaded with him.

"Professor Johansen, you need to put the gun down and thi…" Her voice trailed off, replaced by the low trilling sound of the gun dispatching its deadly answer. The spray pattern from the gun almost cut her in half.

The rest of his colleagues in the control room were hunkered under their stations, some openly weeping while others franticly tried to call for help from their mobile phones to no avail. As Tom executed one by one the people he had only yesterday talked to or discussed the latest theory with while doing the rounds, he could hear his mentor's voice in his head.

"GOOD, TOM, THEY ARE CATTLE. THEY HAVE NO

PLACE IN THE NEW ORDER."

Tom had reached an all-consuming euphoric state by the time he came to his last victim. An older man, Tom thought he was British, a Professor Basford if memory served him right. The professor was calmly leaving a message for his wife when the muzzle of Tom's gun found him. "You will achieve nothing but notoriety by your actions today. Do what you have come to do!" Tom once again squeezed the trigger. His colleague's head exploded like a ripe watermelon sending blood and brain matter across the floor and up the wall. As if to mock the dead, Tom leaned over the professor's body and let out a "moo!" sound, like some bloodthirsty matador who had vanquished his foe in the bullring.

Director Grearson took charge of the situation after hearing the gun fire and explosions. "We need to shut this headcase down before he destroys the facility." The director slipped Bob's gun from its holster and grabbed a couple of radios, which he handed to Jade. Paul surmised that Tom would make use of the collider and his only way of doing that was to take over the main control centre.

Turning to the others, he said, "Follow me." They passed a circular monument known as the Globe of Science and Innovation and headed for the main control centre. As they entered, everything was quiet. The air hung heavy with cordite and death. Glass littered the corridor, then they started finding bodies. The director could only look in horror at the carnage in front of them. "Jesus Christ, I thought Johansen was unbalanced but…" His words tailed of as he recognised the people lying around him. Paul sank to his knees in disbelief. "What if this had been an open day for the public!" Alex put a hand on Paul's shoulder.

"Paul, I know this is hard to swallow but we need to focus,

there is more at stake here than the collider." Alex's words had the desired effect.

"You're right, Alex." Kas and Jade came forward.

"It may be a good idea to split up and cover more ground." Jade was looking directly into Alex's eyes; she knew there was no point in arguing with her.

"Good idea, Jade, you come with me. Kas, you keep an eye on Paul for me." Kas nodded; he had his war head on. Alex thought, 'Good.'

"Is there any floorplan you can give me?" Paul thought for a moment then disappeared and returned with a couple of glossy trifolds.

"We usually keep these for visitors." Paul handed them to Alex.

"Perfect." Alex looked at Paul's handgun.

"Do you know how to use that thing?"

At this point, Paul ejected the magazine, checked it was full, then palmed it back into the hilt of the gun. Next, he slipped the breach back in a quick snapping motion, chambering a round and making the weapon live. "Yes, I've fired the odd round or two." He looked over at Alex who rolled her eyes and smiled.

"Good!"

The director suggested he and Kas continue sweeping through from this end while Alex and Jade reverse tack then move in from the east side of the building.

Alex and Jade entered the east door and followed the map towards the main control room. As they got closer to their goal, the interior of the building became cold and again there was a strong smell of death. Alex slipped the gun out of her belt and ushered Jade behind. Just as they reached the door, Paul snatched a look from the far corner of the hall.

"You guys, okay?" Alex raised her hand and gave Paul a

thumbs-up, then put her palm up, silently asking the director to stay back. Paul nodded his head in agreement.

Alex reached up, taking hold of the door handle and eased the door open. The smell of death poured from the room and was almost overpowering to the point where Alex gagged on reflex. She quickly scanned the room and saw no movement but a lot of dead bodies. After pausing for a few seconds to take stock of what she had just seen, Alex looked over at the director. "I'm pretty sure he's not here but we'll have to check if there has been any damage done, save the obvious, and I'll need you to do that." Paul could not believe the man at lunch was the same person that had killed all these good people. A wave of melancholy swept over him as he looked down at the lifeless faces, all of whom he knew personally.

As he checked each system, words flashed up on the screen; 'INVALID PASSWORD, SYSTEM OVERRIDE'. "The bastard's locked us out!" There was fury in Paul's tone. At that moment, Kas and Jade came to the door. Jade let out a gasp and Alex led her back outside.

"You don't have to see this." Jade nodded; there were tears forming in her eyes. Alex comforted her for a moment then went back into the control room.

On entering the room, something caught her eye at the far right-hand side. There was a flashing red light and as she moved forward, it became more focused. She could see the numbers 00.15, 00.14, 00.13. In that moment, time seemed to slow down. Alex turned to the others, shouting, "BOOOMB!" Everyone instinctively hunkered as they ran.

Alex was last out of the room as the digits continued their unrelenting cascade down to zero. There was a high-pitched whine in their ears as they were all pushed as if by some invisible hand and abruptly stopped by the right-hand wall of the corridor.

"Is everyone ok?" Paul's voice was made rough by the dust that had enveloped the corridor post-explosion. One by one, the others replied with a "Yes!", albeit after a lot of coughing and choking. As the gloom cleared, Alex checked Jade for any injuries; there were none. Leaving Jade's side for a moment, Alex went to the others and looked over them one by one. Apart from some minor cuts, everyone was fine. "A fucking bomb, where the fuck did, he get that!" Paul apologized for swearing. Alex brought them back to the moment.

"It was homemade, a pipe bomb. I'm sure any run-of-the-mill physicist could make one with his eyes closed." There was more than a hint of irony in Alex's words, which wasn't missed by the others. It was the director's turn to speak.

"In a way, I feel personally responsible for all that has happened today." They turned in the direction of Paul who was sitting with his back against the wall. He looked very gaunt and pale. He was about to speak again when Jade interrupted him.

"There is no way we or you can be held responsible for the actions of a deranged mind." She looked at their faces. "I'm sure that I speak for everyone when saying that they and we," Jade pointed back to the office, "are all victims of one man's maniacal scheme." Tears ran down her face, but they were more from anger and frustration. Alex put her hand on Jade's shoulder. As she did this, her eyes focused on the others.

"There will be time later for an inquiry but now in this moment, we have to stop this guy before he does something that will affect things on a global scale." Alex's words echoed not only in the dusty corridor but also in their minds. Kas spoke; he had seen the devastation of the modern weapons and knew that things might get worse.

"This evil man's plan is far reaching, and many lives are at stake. All I need is one chance to end this, and it will be done." Everyone nodded their approval. There was silence for a moment then Paul spoke.

"He'll be heading for the collider's impact chambers and they are underground." Alex looked over at Paul.

"Then lead the way, sir." They walked into bright sunlight and wondered if it would be their last day alive. One thing was certain; Tom Johansen had a fight on his hands.

In the bowels of the CERN facility, Tom was in a state of rapture. "My master is near; my master is near." His words echoed deep within the voids of the collision chamber housing. Tom was setting up his experiment, which he would control by his laptop. His simulations had shown that if he fired in rapid succession with bursts of anti-protons and stored them in the containment unit attached to the collision chamber, he could then release the stored energy through the whole system. Slamming that energy burst into the main collision chamber would create an Einstein-Rosen bridge or wormhole. In doing this, his master could cross to this realm and a new world order would begin. This was his theory. The simulation's figures told Tom it would take a minimum of ten cycles to create enough energy that would allow for his experiment to come alive. Tom ranted constantly as he prepared for the first run. "Soon, soon, then they will know, they will know. Fucking Grearson, I'm in charge, I'm in charge! You will see, you will see, he is coming, he is coming, my lord is coming." He pressed enter, starting the first cycle. "It has beguuun, my looord!" Tom was now panting like some rabid animal, foam gathering in the corners of his mouth. This was a far cry from the bright young scientist that had left Cal Tech Summa Cum Laude, the world his oyster. The whine of the elevator motor hummed into life, bringing Tom back from his ramblings. "I'm afraid this is a closed experiment, no visitors." At this point, Tom picked up the small digital detonator and flipped the switch. As the explosion ripped through the elevator shaft, Tom was screaming at the top of his voice, "SORRY!" He then returned to his laptop and the job at hand.

As they stood waiting on the elevator, Alex was feeling increasingly uneasy. The amulets were beginning to exert their force on her in powerful waves, causing her to feel nauseous. Jade took her arm. "Are you ok? You look awful."

"I thought I was carrying this look off well."

"What look?" Jade was puzzled.

"Scared shitless!" Even in the direst of circumstances, Alex never lost her sense of humour. Jade kissed her on the cheek. Just as she did this, there was a massive rumble from the bowels of the facility. The building shook and the lights went out. The director spoke first.

"Everybody stay calm, the emergency lighting will kick on in a moment." True to his words, the pale blue lighting came on. There was a small stream of smoke coming from the elevator doors that Alex was stood next to.

"I think the mad professor is at his tricks again. The elevator is dead, is there any other way in, Paul?" He thought for a moment.

"There is an emergency exit here." He pointed to his left. "This will get us down to the lower levels." The heavy fire door creaked open sending an echo down the stairwell and into the darkness below. Before going any further, Kas stopped them for a moment.

"I will go first to face what is down there in the belly of this beast. Paul can direct me when we are down at the bottom. Alex, you and Jade can stay behind us, agreed?" By the look on Kas' face, he was not going to take no for an answer. Both Jade and Alex shrugged their shoulders then nodded. Kas seemed to grow another foot in height on their agreeing to let him take point, then started the cautious decent down the staircase into the gloom.

There were no lights on the last three floors to the elevator shaft and that caused concern for all involved. On this occasion, Alex did not have her trusty headtorch, so the decision was made to go forward, albeit carefully. They reached the ground floor; the only light source was through the safety glass in the fire doors. They all peered through the glass before making their way across. Both Paul and Alex took out their guns in anticipation of trouble. Kas got his eye on something and strode forward, pulling it out of its case. It was a fire axe, and his face was beaming. "Where to now, Paul?" Alex tapped the director on the shoulder to get his attention.

"To be honest, Alex, I don't really know. We will just have to be systematic."

They ventured deeper into the underworld labyrinth containing pipes, wires, and machinery. It began to feel like they were in the bowels of some massive space craft. The unfortunate circumstance was that Paul knew this strange environment, but the others were out of their depth, quite literally, which meant they could not split up and cover more ground. Paul directed Kas forward, checking each room as they came upon them. They rounded a corner and saw a dark tunnel off to their left. Immediately Kas darted inside, disappearing into the blackness.

As Kas felt his way about in the darkness, he became aware of another presence with him. This presence was so strong that Kas had to stop to try and clear his head. At this moment, he started to feel nauseous, and a booming voice started pounding on his senses.

In the corridor, Alex, Jade, and Paul were becoming increasingly worried about Kas but they could not call out in case they warned Tom of their presence. The first thing Alex noticed about Kas when he reappeared was his eyes; they were void of emotion. Kas held the fire axe rigid and close to his body. Alex laughed, unconsciously being reminded of Jack Nicholson's portrayal of Jack Torrance in the movie 'The Shining'. "Kas, Kas!" Alex spoke to her friend but got no response. She was about to say his name again when Kas finally replied but the voice that came out sounded nothing like their friend.

"YOU WILL GIVE ME THE KEY!" Alex immediately knew the voice and so did Jade.

"Paul, you need to get behind us, NOW!" The director knew by their tone that the situation had just gotten serious and moved back. Their friend was nothing more than a mere puppet in the hands of the Darkness.

"Kas, you need to come back to us." Kas moved forward.

"That won't help you, your friend belongs to me now." Anger grew in the pit of Alex's stomach. She knew the only way to get her friend back was to incapacitate him, but how? Jade spoke next.

"Do you remember me, filth?" Kas' head snapped around as he focused his attention on Jade.

"Hello, my dear, I'm looking forward to having a lot of fun with you." Jade engaged Kas as Alex edged her way further up the corridor, trying to blindside her foe and get Kas back. Alex caught the shoulder movement first, which was fortunate for her as the axe thundered into the wall not two feet in front of her.

"Going somewhere?" Alex's foe taunted her as it recovered the axe from the wall.

"Well, it's been really nice catching up but back to business, THE KEY." The creature's voice hit them with immense force. Alex checked on Jade.

"You, okay?" Jade nodded. "Where's Paul?" They both

looked around but there was no sign of the director.

Kas moved towards his friends, axe at the ready. As he pulled it back to strike the first blow, he stopped. All the air seemed to leave his lungs and he toppled forward. Standing in his place was Director Grearson.

"These power freaks talk a load of crap!" He tucked the gun back into his waistband. Jade ran forward and kissed him while Alex shook his hand.

"You're full of surprises, Paul." Grearson shrugged his shoulders.

"I've had dealings with his type all my life, they always talk a good shop." A large grin broke across his face and across the others'.

After a couple of minutes, Kas began to stir. His instinct was to get up, but Alex and Jade restrained him, not wanting their friend to hurt himself. "What happened and why is my head aching?" As Kas spoke, his eyes were squinting, mostly because of the knock on the head he had received from Paul but also to gain focus again. Jade told him about the Darkness taking control of his body. Kas found it hard to believe as he thought his force of will was strong enough to stop such an attack. Slowing getting to his feet, Kas leaned against the wall till he got his bearings. "Who hit me on the head?" Alex and Jade looked at each other then slowly turned and faced Paul.

"Thanks, guys, never heard of pointing elbows?" Paul laughed. "I'm sorry, Kas, but trying to negotiate with a demigod always ends in tears." Kas walked over to Paul and took him by the shoulders.

"You are now my warrior kin the same as Alex and Jade. I will repay your courage with my loyalty." Paul smiled. He wondered why Kas spoke like he did but put that to one side and thanked him for being so understanding about things. "If everyone is ok, will we find the good Professor Johansen."

As if on cue, the facilities PA crackled into life.

"Fee-fi-fo-fum, I smell the blood of an Englishman, be he alive or be he dead, I'll crush his bones to make my bread." It was obvious that Tom's train had left and had gone to 'Crazyville'.

He called out, "Hey Grearson, who's in charge now? You're a politician, not a true scientist like me, but fear not, my new master will show you the error of your ways." The PA snapped off, sending an echo down into the depths.

"We need to find him quickly. I've got a bad feeling about this, and I never ignore my gut instinct." Alex's whole persona had gone still as if she were going into a state of 'no mind' or what his martial arts teachers would call 'mushin'. It was the Japanese concept of emptying one's mind to free the body and allow it to respond in the moment, and Jade had seen this before when Alex had fought Braunn.

Paul moved forward carefully. They continued to check each room as they went, not wanting to rush ahead and possibly miss something important. The director stopped suddenly, turning to the others.

"I think he is in the collision housing; the system is running, and it seems a logical step given the experiment he planned." Paul gave everyone a rough idea of the layout in the collision housing; unfortunately, there was only one entrance, but there were four of them which surely would give them the edge.

Tom had fallen deep into the pit of insanity. He looked at his laptop which read '50%'. "Halfway point. Now to deal with the spoilers."

Chapter Thirty

Paul put his hand up signaling for the others to stop. He motioned to Alex to come and look at something. Alex tracked Paul's finger which was pointing at a spot about twenty meters ahead where there was a small red light barely visible in the gloom. If the main lights had been on, it would have not shown up in the glare. "Is that what I think it is?" Alex took her eyes off the small red light.

"Yes, it's an IED (Improvised Explosive Device), well spotted." They discussed their options, the P.A. system crackled into life.

"He is coming, he is coming, my master is near, and you will become fodder for the new order." The speaker snapped off. Alex was first to talk.

"This guy is gone, and we have to recognize that." She looked at the faces around her as they waited for her to continue. "If we have to take his life, it is in the safe knowledge that he is putting the planet at risk or at least most of Europe with the course he's on." The friends all understood the gravity of the situation. They pulled their attention back to the task at hand, examining the device at the safest possible distance. It was agreed that there was not a remote detonation system on the bomb, which left a few options; vibration activation, some sort of trip wire, or a beam trigger system.

After pondering the situation for a few moments, Alex asked Paul, "Is it a dry wall down here?" Paul thought for a moment.

"There's only one way to find out." He shrugged his shoulders, which gave Alex the green light to try out her theory. Alex went back down the corridor and into one of the side rooms. She went up to the wall and tapped it; there was a hollow reply. Taking a step backwards to get the correct distance, Alex lunged forward, putting her right foot through the wall. In doing so, it also answered her question.

"We can bypass the device in the corridor by going through these two dry walls." Alex pointed into the room they were standing next to. "Does anyone have a sharp knife?" Not surprising to Alex, Kas pulled out a short blade.

"Will this do?"

"Perfect," said Alex, "Where did you get this?"

"Found it lying around."

"Really, Kas, we have talked about this." After taking the knife off Kas, Alex went into the room, cleared a space where she needed and etched a large cross on the wall. She then put her shoulder against it and pushed. The wall gave way along the lines that Alex had marked. Alex and the others then quickly cleared the rubble and repeated the process on the adjacent wall. As luck would have it, there were neither wires nor conduits for water hidden in the wall so their passage into the next room was relatively easy. Alex checked the room doorway for any beam that may trigger the device.

"I think if we go through this wall, we should be clear to continue in the main corridor." Once again, they repeated what they had done previously, though this time having to navigate some power cables, but they made good progress. Back in the main corridor, Paul warned the others that they were approaching the collider housing.

"This is the only door in and out so we will need to be vigilant on entering. There is a lot of cover behind workstations and the machinery that supports the collider."

Reading '80%', Tom's laptop told him it was nearly time to warm up Atlas, the smaller accelerator, prior to transferring the mass body of energy to the main loop. He typed in the word 'Execute' and pressed the enter key on the laptop. At this point, Tom's focus was pulled to the noise from further down the corridor. 'My little surprise will keep them at bay,' he thought to himself, laughing out loud as he did.

Alex returned through the improvised doors with a powder fire extinguisher in her hands. "Thought this could be our way into the chamber!"

"Good thinking, Alex, that will be a perfect distraction." Paul was fired up. He did not like the idea of some madman running among this multi-billion-euro facility, not on his watch.

The collider housing was a massive room and like most of the mechanical innards at CERN there were vast arrays of pipes, wires and conduits carrying everything from electricity to supercooled helium. The collision chamber itself took up most of one side of the complete area. There was a red warning light flashing, indicating that an experiment was on going. Tom worked at his laptop on a workstation next to the collider. He looked totally disheveled; his hair was a mess, the tail of his shirt hung outside the suit trousers.

Tom worked at a fast pace; he could feel a strange vibration that he'd never felt before while running the experiment. He thought it must be an overlooked factor of the mass of energy being contained within, but at that moment, Tom began to feel nauseous – not unlike the feeling the others felt when being transported from one realm to the other. When he looked back to his laptop it read '95%' and Tom's gut instinct was giving him alarm bells. He ignored it, thinking more about his master's arrival.

Whilst he was lost in his thoughts, the main door burst open, and the room filled with smoke. Tom turned and sprayed the doorway with rounds from his MP5. There was the sound of ricochets everywhere and someone cried out in the gloom.

Tom thought, 'No, no, no!' as he pulled the trigger again. There was a loud click. "Shit!" He'd ran out of ammunition for the machine gun but quickly grabbed for one of the two 9mms tucked into his belt. After bringing it forward in the direction of the door, he flipped the safety from red to green and listened intently for any noise.

Kas had been hit through the shoulder by one of Tom's bullets. Jade looks at the wound. "I think it's a through and through, we just need to pack it." Jade tended his injury as Kas asked her what had hit him.

"Was that an arrow? I have been hit by an arrow, but it did not feel like this." Jade had no time to explain to Kas what a bullet was, so she told him it was a special arrow that moved quickly.

Everyone felt the pull of Tom's portal, now so familiar, and knew they did not have much time. Alex could hear the Darkness; it was close, she could feel it in every heartbeat, like a drum of doom pounding in her chest. At this point, she talked directly to Tom. "Professor Johansen, my name is Alex McDonald and I need to talk to you."

"Save your breath, highlander, my master has told me about you." Tom's voice was beginning to sound oh-so-familiar to Alex; he sounded like the Darkness. Alex changed tack.

"Did your master tell you about the amulets of power and what he intends to do with them?" There was a long silence before Tom spoke again.

"My master has no need for these charms of power for I have given him THIS CRUCIBLE OF POWER." Alex could see through the gloom that Tom was spinning around with his arms raised like some maniacal version of 'The Sound of Music'.

Paul called to Alex, "What is it, Paul?" She asked.

The director brought Alex's attention to the area next to

the collider.

"If I'm not mistaken, that looks like a temporal distortion or gate." Alex told him. The side of the collider had become translucent, almost like looking into a pool of water. Every now and again, a ripple drifted across it making it feel like it could come alive at any moment. Paul grabbed Alex's arm firmly.

"That's a Rosen bridge. That cannot be possible but there it is." Alex wanted to tell Paul about the gateways to the realms but felt now was not the time.

"Is that like a wormhole?" Alex played dumb but felt like she was lying to Paul. The director was transfixed for a moment before answering Alex.

"Yes, you're right, a wormhole." Paul could not really get things processing correctly due to the magnitude of what was before him. Alex brought him to earth, albeit with a bump.

"Well, your buddy is trying to destroy us and possibly the rest of the world. We need to destroy it, but first Tom has to be taken out and quickly." On the other side of the passageway, Jade had managed to rig a field dressing to Kas' shoulder wound. "How's the big guy doing?" Alex called over to Jade.

"He's doing fine," she said with her thumbs up.

The next thing Alex said she did by signaling with her hands. Pointing to herself and Paul, she then drew two half circles in the air, finally finishing by making finger guns and nodded her head in the direction of Tom. Jade smiled and gave him the thumbs up. Alex drew Tom into a talk about the bridge.

"Professor Johansen, how did you do it, create a wormhole? Aren't you out of your depth in this field and how do you know it will stabilize?" Alex was buying time for Paul to get into position, which he nearly was. Then Alex would make her own move. Tom wondered what Alex knew about wormholes.

"What's your field of study, highlander?" With a little smile on his face, Alex knew that Tom was about to go ballistic.

"My field of study is geology." Tom exploded into a rant.

"YOU'RE A FUCKING ROCK CRACKER, THAT'S JUST FUCKING GREAT. YOU THINK SOMEONE OF YOUR LOW-GRADE TALENT CAN TAKE AWAY MY GREATEST ACHIEVEMENT? JUST GO, TAKE YOUR FRIENDS AND CRAWL BACK UNDER WHATEVER ROCK TAKES YOUR FUCKING FANCY AND DIE!"

As Tom ranted, Paul took up position on his right with Alex on his left. Just before Tom started to talk again, Alex replied to her original statement.

"Yes, I crack rocks." 'And heads,' Alex thought, then continued. "But unlike you, I can prove my research by having tangible evidence that what happened or what is going to happen will come about within a certain time frame, not just a bunch of numbers and accusations of a so-called theory." With a quick look down at his laptop and seeing '98%', Tom replied in a quieter and more threatening tone.

"You're about to meet one of my theories."

Alex and Paul looked at the void which had become increasingly dark, but now there was movement in the blackness; they knew time was short. On a count of three, Alex rose first then Paul, both flipping their safeties off. With guns supported in both hands, they brought them to bear on Tom's position, but he was not there.

"Shit." As Alex tried to re-acquire where Tom was, a bullet ripped through her thigh. Alex let out a roar of pain. Paul brought his gun around and managed to hit Tom in the arm, but it was just a graze. Tom squeezed his trigger, missing Paul's head by mere inches, then there was silence. The smell of gunpowder hung in the air and the odd grunt of pain disturbed a deathly silence. Jade called out to Alex.

"Are you alright?" Silence. She was about to shout again

when she heard Alex's voice call out.

"I'm fine, just a nick," she lied. Alex had used her handkerchief and belt to make a pressure bandage which had managed to stop the bleeding, but she was still in some considerable pain. Tom voice called out across the room.

"Highlander, have you lost something?" Alex was confused then she heard Jade's voice.

"Alex don't let himmm…" Her words were lost as Tom put his hand back across her mouth. Alex sat trying to think of a way to get Jade back safely. Tom spoke again.

"Think I'll keep this one, she's a screamer." Tom started to laugh then he looked at the screen again. That was a mistake.

Kas was furious. He picked up his axe and waited for his chance. He did not have to wait long; the mad sorcerer was looking at his spell and Kas rose, covering the ground between himself and Tom in no time. Swinging the fire axe up over his shoulder, Kas buried the pointed end deep into Tom's thigh. This had the instant effect of releasing Jade, who Kas caught and in one smooth motion took her back to the safety of the workstations.

Tom was in agony but still managed to get a round off in Kas' direction, but it buried itself in the wall above the warrior's head. Watching all of this, Paul and Alex took their cue from Kas' heroics and shot the gun out of Tom's hand and wounded him in his other leg, which left Tom lying in a pathetic heap on the floor. "I am just his messenger, he," Tom pointed to the dark void which was growing bigger with every second, "will bring destruction to your miserable lives." Tom passed out with the pain.

"What do we do to stop this, Professor Grearson?" Paul stood motionless for the briefest of moments; no one had called him professor in quiet some time, but he came back to his thoughts quickly.

"We need to disrupt the anti-protons in some way, hopefully then we can use the rest of the smaller colliders to vent off enough energy to shut that thing down." Paul pointed to the void. Just as he did, a voice bellowed across from the nether world; it was one word – 'Highlander'. Taking the small bag off her shoulder, Alex asked Paul,

"What if I added base metals like gold into the chamber? Would that have any effect on the process?" Again, for a moment Paul was quiet then he said the simplest of things; "It's worth a try."

They went to the main body of the collider and Paul showed Alex where she could put the gold. It was a small aluminum tube that could be placed in the chamber by a robotic arm. Alex took out the cylinder and without a second thought placed it inside the small tube, then Paul put the tube in the applicator and shut the door. The robotic arm moved smoothly inside its housing, picking up the tube then placing it in the chute that led directly into the heart of the collider. Paul looked at the void then at Alex. "If you're going to do it, I suggest you do it now." Alex hit the green button, sending the projectile into the collider. The black void immediately bulged outwards quite considerably. Then came the voice of the Darkness.

"Another time, McDonald, anoth…"

The room returned to normal. The void was gone, and everyone gathered in front of the collider. As they stood together, they checked each other's war wounds and did what they could to tend to them. They were preparing to leave when Paul stopped everyone. "We may have a small problem." The collider's heat shield was at critical, and they needed to vent the excess energy through the smaller chambers, but they would have to do it sequentially. Paul took the others and put them on a workstation, showing them what to do when he asked them. All this time, the emergency lights flashed constantly and as if it could not get worse, a mechanical voice cracked into life on the PA.

"Imminent core failure in one-minute, imminent core failure in one minute, immin…"

Alex emptied the rest of the clip from her gun into the speaker on the wall then turned to the others.

"Sorry but this is stressful enough," she said then shrugged her shoulders. Everyone shook their heads. Paul stood at the main console.

"On my mark and starting with you, Kas." The warrior looked up at Paul. "Now!" Kas did as he was shown, then Alex and finally Jade. Everything was still flashing. Paul turned to them. "We may have been too late. I'm sorry, my friends." They all came together in the centre of the room. Alex looked around at the faces before her then spoke.

"If I could choose who I wanted to die with, then you guys would be it." She then turned to Jade. "You have completed me in so many ways that I can't begin to say, least only that you know that I love you and would have spent the rest of my life with you." She kissed Jade softly on the lips.

All Jade could say in reply was, "Ditto." They stood together as they had fought together, as one. Then it happened; the emergency lights blinked off one by one.

They all turned to Paul, who said with more than a sense of relief, "WE DID IT!" There was a lot of hugging and kissing as they came to realise that they were going to survive. Returning their attention to Tom, Jade asked,

"What are we going to do about him?" Paul looked at Alex.

"We will leave him for the authorities to deal with." They all nodded their approval.

The friends went back into the corridor, through the improvised doors and were about to head for the stairs when they heard Tom's voice. He must have managed to crawl out of the control room and into the corridor.

"You think you have won but this is only one war, he will be back." Tom turned and looked at the red light on the IED then shuffled forward into the beam. The others realised what he was doing and ran for the stairs as the device exploded sending them all hurtling into the fire doors.

Chapter Thirty-One

There is a soft hum as the hospital room's air conditioning came to life. The metronomic *ping* of heart monitors as they competed with one another was the only other noise in an otherwise peaceful room. Alex lay asleep, a pulse oximeter sat on one finger with a drip canula, and stand attached to her other arm. Her eyes opened and she let them adjust to the light. In the bed adjacent, Jade's smiling face greeted her as she sat up in a more comfortable position. "Hi!" Alex whispered to Jade. She looked at the bed diagonally across from her where Kas lay unconscious. "How's the big guy doing?" Jade smiled.

"He's fine, a severe concussion but they say he'll be feeling better in a or two."

Jade hoped out of bed and made her way to Alex's side. She poured her a glass of water then sat on the bed with a huge grin on her face. "Your headache should be OK in a couple of hours, doc said we're all blessed to come out of this with the injuries we have." Jade rubbed Alex's leg, she winced. "Sorry, forgot you got nicked by that bullet, you'll be on crutches for a bit."

"Aye that'll be right." Alex scoffed. "Anyway, what's your excuse for being in here with us genuine sick folk?" Jade laughed.

"Mild concussion and some cuts and abrasions. The doctor wants me under observation since its technically a brain injury." It was Alex's turn to laugh, which she regretted, holding her head then drinking again. She took Jade's hand.

"Joking aside, I'm glad you're OK, that we're all OK, have you seen Paul?" Jade smiled.

"Yes, he's fine, sore leg and a headache, said he'd pop by later."

"Good, as I was saying, I'm glad we put a stop to Tom's madness, maybe he'll fine some peace now that he's gone." Jade nodded. She reached over and kissed Alex. The door opened and there was a polite cough as Paul Grearson entered walking with a cane.

"Hope I'm not disturbing anything." Jade and Alex laugh.

"Nothing that can't wait, how's the leg?" Paul sat on the other side of Alex's bed.

"It's fine, the stick's just a precaution. How's the food?"

"Intravenous." Alex grinned and held up her arm. Paul smiled.

"I hear Kas will be OK in a few days, brave man, he bore the brunt of the explosion." They sat quiet for a moment. "Anyway, back to business. I've spoken to the authorities, and they are willing to take written statements from you as a way of tying any loose ends up with regards what happened. I hold some clout given my position so there will be no need for anyone to go before the bar." Alex squeezed his arm gently.

"Thanks Paul. I think it's best that we try to move on from this terrible chapter in our lives, I've had my fill to be quite honest." Jade took her hand.

"Yeah, me too Paul. I'm very grateful for what you've done for us all and will be eternally grateful for all your help." She reached over and kissed his cheek. Paul blushed.

"Thank you my dear, but we all know who the true heroes are." He looked at them one-by-one. "And you'll have the scares to prove it." He stood letting the cane take his weight.

"I've arranged for a private plane to transport you home when you are all able to take that journey. All I ask of you my dears is that you take the proper time to heal and enjoy some off the delights that Geneva has to offer." Alex took his hand again; she pulled him close and kissed his cheek holding him there for a moment.

"I knew a man once, he was kind, brave and honest, just like you." She kissed him once again and let go of his arm. As Paul stood, he brushed a tear from his eye then took out his handkerchief and blew his nose.

"You're to kind." He smiled. Paul walked to the door. "I'll be back before you go, maybe we could have dinner?"

"That would be nice Paul." Jade replied.

"You'll have to come to visit us, when we get back home." Jade called out.

"It would be my pleasure; I've heard your country is beautiful." He smiled one last time, with that he left.

Chapter Thirty-Two

A pristine blue sky blanketed the snow covered the peaks of the mountains as if nature herself had personally framed this moment for those who looked on. Mountain streams percolated through narrow fissures in the rock creation their own unique symphony as they cascaded their way to the valley floor. A myriad of blooms, flora and fauna carpet the bare rock, claiming their right to life in this beautiful but sometimes harsh environment. Familiar voices invade the stillness of this serine and awe-inspiring landscape. They laugh and giggle playfully with one another till finally Alex and Jade crest the first ridge. A few paces behind, Kas looked up to the two women and shook his head. "I'm afraid our friend is not built for this environment he would be left to tend the children back home." Jade and Alex laughed.

"That's a bit harsh Kas, surely he could be more use than a nursemaid?" Jade asked.

"Maybe in this world, back home we may even leave him in the wood at night as an offering to our gods." He laughed at his last statement, as did Jade and Alex.

"Paul, Kas is berating your good name, you need to get yer arse in gear and come up here to sort him out." Paul Grearson puts his hands on his knees and gulps lungs full of mountain air.

"Whatever he's saying, it's true. I'm not built for this kind of terrain…" Kas Smiles. "To many years stuck behind a desk have left my muscles built for the sprint and not to do battle with gravity." The others laugh.

"Not long now Paul, we're nearly there, then we can show you the big surprise." Alex waves Paul up the path, then she and the others walk out of sight.

"Not long now old chap, then we can have a rest." Paul starts to climb all be at a vastly reduced speed than the others.

Paul finally reached the top of the ridge, before him the lost valley in all its splendor. "My goodness, what a sight to behold, it's breathtaking, simple breathtaking." Alex called up from further down the track.

"Was it worth the effort Paul?" Still trying to catch his breath he called back to her.

"I was just saying to myself…its breathtaking, in more ways than one." Paul giggled to himself.

"Hey, old man we have something to show you, if you can manage to get down here before day turns to night." Kas looked sternly at Paul then started to laugh.

"You're really embracing the Scottish humour Kas." He nodded his agreement. Paul made his way down till finally the friends stood beneath the huge form of the sentry. He looked up at the majestic rock. "I know you said you had a surprise, but this is just stunning. To think a glacier millennia ago, move this beast to this spot is simple beyond belief, but here it stands." The friends nodded in unison.

"Yeah, you're right it is amazing, but that's not the surprise." Alex looked at the faces of her friends. "Fate brought us together and only fate can undo our kinship born out of necessity." Paul nodded.

Alex takes out her grandfather's watch, she opens it like she's done a thousand times previously but now there's a greater significance to this simple of actions. She looks around at the smiling faces before her and knows she has finally come home. Jade reached out to Paul and nodded to Kas to join them, which he did. "Paul we couldn't think of a gift that would do justice for the kindness and support you have shown us in our short time together." Paul smiled, albeit slightly bemused.

Jade continued. "So, this is a combined gift from us all, but mostly from Alex and her kin who have guarded this secret for centuries." Jade nods to Alex. She walked to the base of the great boulder, placing her watch in the appropriate hole, and stepped back. She joined hands with the others and looked directly at Paul.

"You know something Paul, Einstein was right, there are other worlds." She smiled as they disappeared through the portal.

THE END